"Would you like to see it?" I ask him. "The painting. Would you like to see it?"

"Sure."

"Well. You have to come over here."

He seems to come out of his daze and walk over to me.

He stops right in front of me, his eyes never leaving mine. "It's beautiful."

I smile. "You haven't even looked at it yet."

"I don't have to see it to know. I already know it's lovely."

I shrug and dab my paint brush into a mix of white and blue, making an even lighter blue. One that matches the color of his eyes.

I touch the paint lightly to the canvas, turning a dot of paint into the image of a pale blue wildflower.

"You make it look so easy," he says.

I glance up. He's watching me paint now.

"Do you paint?" I ask.

"No. But I appreciate art. And you have talent."

"You know art?"

"I spent a fair amount of time in the Museum of Fine Arts in Boston."

"I'm impressed." I dab more flowers onto the page, mostly because he seems to like them. "And surprised."

He looks back at me now, with a little smile on his lips. "You don't expect to meet anyone out here who appreciates art."

"I rarely meet anyone anywhere who appreciates art."

"I find that very sad."

"It is sad."

"You must be Wyatt," I say, adding some green paint to my brush.

"And you must be Lilah."

"Impressed and surprised once more."

"My brother is in love with your sister and your name has come up."

"I knew she was wrong," I say, stepping back to study my canvas.

"Who was wrong about what?"

"Audrey. She thinks Bradley is just here temporarily. To protect her."

"Sometimes it takes a minute to figure those things out."

"Sometimes," I say, meeting his gaze again.

"Sometimes not."

Something in those blue eyes tug at me and tell me we aren't talking about our siblings any more.

"What's that?" I ask. "Under your arm."

"What?" He seems to have forgotten he was holding something. He pulls it out and glances at it. "Security camera to keep you safe."

"Are you supposed to be installing it?" I glance past him. "Bradley's on his way out here with a ladder."

"Right. Yes." He doesn't look away. "Will you have dinner with me? Tonight?"

"Okay," I say, more than little amused.

"And tomorrow night?"

"I don't know. Aren't we supposed to see how tonight goes?"

"Who makes these rules?"

"I don't know."

"Wyatt," Bradley calls. "Where do you want me to put the ladder?"

"I have to go. I'll pick you up at six."

As he walks away to join his brother, I remember with a bit of annoyance at myself that it was only days ago that I vowed to myself to never date again.

JUST SURFACE

THE GRAVITY OF US SERIES

KATHRYN KALEIGH

The Gravity of Us Series

(Reading Order)

Just Breathe

Just Surface

Just Melt

All of the books in the Gravity of Us Series are

standalone and can be read out of order.

However, the books are best when read in order.

ALSO BY KATHRYN KALEIGH

The Gravity of Us Series

(Reading Order)

Just Breathe

Just Surface

Just Melt

Standalone Suspense

Out of Ashes

~ CONTEMPORARY ~

Alpine Falls (Maybe Yours) Series

(Reading Order)

Still Yours (Maybe)

Yours for Christmas (Maybe)

Forever Yours (Maybe)

(ALPINE FALLS)

Stranded in Alpine Falls

Belonging in Alpine Falls

The Spirit of Christmas in Alpine Falls

Christmas Wishes in Alpine Falls

Finding True North in Alpine Falls

A Ghost of Christmas Magic in Alpine Falls

Secrets and Second Chances

Honeymoon with a Stranger

Not Our Wedding

(SILVER PINES)

The Way Back to You

Back to Where We Began

When We Were Us

(ONCE UPON FOREVER)

My Forever Guy

Our Forever Love

Forever Vows

Finding Forever

Accidentally Forever

(TRUE NORTH)

Borrowed Until Monday

Still Mine

The Moon and the Stars at Christmas

Perfectly Mismatched

On the Way to Forever

A Merry Little Christmas

On the Way Home to Christmas

It was Always You

(UNBREAK MY HEART)

Begin Again

Love Again

Falling Again

(FOR THE LOVE OF THE FLIGHT)

Just Stay

Just Chance

Just Believe

Just Us

Just Once

Just Happened

Just Maybe

Just Pretend

Just Because

(MAGNETIC NORTH)

Second Chance Kisses

Second Chance Secrets

First Time Charm

Three Broken Rules

Second Chance Destiny

Unexpected Vows

(FALLING FOR CHRISTMAS)

The Heart of Christmas

The Magic of Christmas

In a One Horse Open Sleigh

A Secret Royal Christmas

An Old Fashioned Christmas

(CITY SKYLINE BILLIONAIRES)

Billionaire's Unexpected Landing

Billionaire's Accidental Girlfriend

Billionaire's Fallen Angel

Billionaire's Secret Crush

Billionaire's Barefoot Bride

(TRULY, MADLY, DEEPLY)

The Lady in the Red Dress

On the Edge of Chance

Sealed with a Kiss

Kiss Me at Midnight

The Heart Knows

(STOLEN ECHOES)

When Cupid's Arrow Strikes

Chasing Fireflies

A Chance Encounter

(EDGE OF THE HORIZON)

The Forever Equation

Pretend Boyfriend

All our Tomorrows

Kissing for Keeps

Out of the Blue

The Princess and the Playboy

(RED LIPSTICK KISSES)

Red Lipstick Kisses and Small Town Wishes

Stolen Dances and Big City Chances

Chance Connections and Upside Down Plans

A Christmas Kiss on the Twenty-Fifth

Believe in the Magic of Christmas

Vows of Inheritance Series

(Reading Order)

Vow to Protect

Vow to Redeem

ROMANTASY

(IN THE SPIRIT OF LOVE)

Spirits of the Heart

Out of Dreams and Ashes

Etched Upon the Heart

WESTERN ROMANCE

(LONE STAR HEARTS)

Wanted by a Texas Ranger

Saved by a Texas Ranger

(WHISKEY SPRINGS)

Finding Natalie

Promising Samantha

Falling for Allyson

Saving Savannah

Claiming Charlie

Rescuing Keira

Protecting Gabriella

Courting Isabella

TIME TRAVEL

(INTO THE MIST)

Written in the Wind

Scripted in the Stars

Destined in the Twilight

Promised in the Mist

Trapped in the Melody

(DRAGON'S BLOOD)

Dragon's Blood

Lavender Blue

Champagne Silver

Twilight Frost

Mountbatten Pink

(WHEN HEARTSTRINGS BECKON)

Rescued in Time

Meet me in 1879

(WHEN HEARTSTRINGS ECHO)

Messages Across Time

Falling Through to Forever

Once Upon a Winter's Spell

(BECKONED)

Before the Storm

Twist of Fate

When the Stars Align

Once Upon a Christmas

Once in a Blue Moon

A Wish Upon a Star

(BEGUILED)

When Lightning Strikes

Storm of Time

Midnight Storm

When the Moon Falls

Stormborn Angel

(SPELLED)

Time Tempest

The Heart Remembers

A Moment in Time

Moonlight Shadows

HISTORICAL

(TAPESTRY OF BLUE AND GRAY)

Shadows Beneath Magnolia Blooms

Secrets Among Southern Roses

(IT HAPPENED BY ACCIDENT)

Accidentally Alluring

Accidentally Married

(SOUTHERN BELLE CIVIL WAR)

Beyond Enemy Lines

Love Always

Hearts Under Siege

Hearts Under Fire

Away Down South in Dixie

The Reluctant Bride

Stay with Me

Jasmine Kisses

Magnolia Kisses

Gardenia Kisses

(THE QUINNS)

Wait for Me

Take Me Home

Keep Me Safe

FATED MATES

Riley's Mate

Aiden's Mate

Brayden's Mate

STANDALONE SUSPENSE

JUST SURFACE

Lilah Sinclair
Houston, Texas

I WOULD HAVE BEEN BETTER off taking a job as a showgirl.

Not that I knew any dance moves.

And learning choreographed dance moves would definitely have been more challenging than learning how to mix a Paper Plane cocktail and knowing the nuances of how that's different from the Last Word cocktail.

As a bartender, I'm not only required to know how to mix every possible drink, but also know a little bit of the history of each one. For example, the Last Word is a pre-

Prohibition cocktail that has suddenly become popular again.

People like it when their bartender can give them factual information. I only make it up about ten, maybe twenty percent of the time.

If I don't know how to mix a drink or some interesting fact about one, and I have time, my good friend Perplexity can help me out.

Fortunately, I have an excellent memory and I never have to look anything up more than once. So far. That, I am certain, is destined to change, simply because there are over ten thousand distinct mixed drinks.

Not to mention wines, beers, and spirits.

I work at two different bars. When I go in, I go all in. Besides, no point in not squeezing the most out of everything I'm learning about alcoholic drinks.

Tonight I'm at the Hobby Center. Only open when there is a Broadway event. Opening nights, like this, are my favorite. I love the elegance. The richness. The sophistication of it all.

With a tray of drinks in hand, I head off to deliver them to a group of well-dressed people who were standing in the far corner near the window when I left them.

I weave my way unobtrusively among the other patrons. Like moving furniture. No one notices the servers.

I find my group of three women and three men easily

enough. Separately, they all look stunning, but together, they make an unforgettable picture. The men are wearing black-tie tuxedos and the ladies are wearing sparkly evening gowns. All in their twenties, about my age.

And yet they obviously come from a world I can only dream of being part of.

There was a time when I somehow thought I would

I have no misperceptions that I landed this particular job at the Hobby Center in downtown Houston based on my bartending skills.

They hired me because I make people look twice.

No one notices the servers. Until they do.

I'm not particularly tall. An average five six. One hundred fifteen pounds. Long, healthy blonde hair that I'm supposed to wear loose around my shoulders when I'm out on the floor.

My work uniform is a black form-fitting cocktail dress. Very tasteful with a high neck and long sleeves. I've been told I wear it well.

I've even been told that I have a rich girl look, whatever that means. I assume it means my figure. Maybe a combination of my figure and my straight hair with just a hint of curl on the ends.

It helps that I have a ready smile. I sometimes wonder where I got that.

The figure and hair I come by honest. Both my sisters have a similar build with similar hair. My oldest sister has more of a serious sultry look and the middle sister wears a perpetual vexed expression that men, for some reason, find sexy.

I definitely came out ahead with my ready smile, in my humble opinion.

This particular group ordered champagne. Their loss and no challenge for me.

Holding my tray on one arm, I hand out glasses of champagne with my free hand.

Moving furniture.

The women take their flutes without bothering to acknowledge me. The men give me quick glances, artfully designed to not make their girlfriends or wives jealous.

I don't care. This is just a job for me.

"Hey," the slightly plump girl with blonde streaks says to me just as I lower my tray and start turning to leave.

I look at her with a pleasant, questioning smile.

She doesn't look the least bit familiar to me and she shouldn't. I've worked here for three months and I've only recognized a repeat customer a couple of times.

Honestly, they would recognize me before I would recognize them.

"Can I bring you something else?" I ask politely.

"You look familiar. Lily? Layla?"

"Lilah," I correct, feeling an unease creep along my spine. We don't wear name tags and there's no reason for this young woman to recognize me.

"Yes. That's it."

As though I don't know my own name. But I keep my

expression schooled in politeness. "Enjoy your evening," I say, starting to turn again.

"Didn't you date Trey?"

How could she possibly know this? "I think you have the wrong person." There's a time for honesty and there's a time for most definitely not admitting to something. This is the latter.

"No," she insists.

"Bernice," the man next to her says in a warning tone. "Let it go."

But Bernice does not appear inclined to let anything go.

"He told me about you."

"Enjoy your evening," I say again and this time I do turn around.

"He said you're a little too clingy for his taste."

Two steps away, I stop. My heart is beating like a jackhammer. But I take deep breaths and count to ten.

The man murmurs something to her.

She's had too much to drink. It happens. There's no need for me to take offense. I don't even know this woman and she has no reason to know me despite knowing my name and that I dated Trey for all of five minutes.

But Bernice follows me. I *feel* her following me. *Hear* her heels clicking on the marble floor behind me.

Then I sense her breath as she walks up behind me.

"Trey told me that you're a good lay, but you'll never

be more than that. Someone to just fuck when he feels like it. But he said he's not a garbage collector and you're just trash—"

I'll never really be able to explain what happened after that.

All I know is that I turn around, my fingers closing around the stem of a glass of red wine from the man standing nearest me and tossing it. I just toss it and the deep crimson liquid sails through the air. Right across Bernice's smug elegantly painted face.

Her gasp is sharp and wet, the wine dripping from her chin, running down her neck, and blooming in red blotches across her white silk blouse.

CHAPTER
TWO

Lilah

HALF AN HOUR LATER, I'm sitting in Natalie's office. Natalie is the boss. The big boss. Vice-President big boss. I normally would have to go through three other bosses to get to her kind of big boss. I don't think she was even here. I'm pretty sure they called her in. For this. For me.

My heart is still pounding faster than is natural, but I keep my gaze down.

I'm in a precarious situation and I know it.

Twenty minutes later, Natalie, in her perfect light blue trim business suit walks in and leans against her wooden desk.

"Please tell me you have a good explanation for what happened," she says. She stares at me, her lips pressed tightly together.

"I—" I clear my throat and try again. "I do."

But Natalie doesn't seem to hear me. "I know it wasn't an accident. It's on camera. Do you want to see the footage?"

I shake my head. I really, really, really do not want to relive the moment.

Less than one hour. It only took one hour for my life to be flipped upside down.

"Do you know the definition of assault?"

I look up at her then, searching her eyes for some semblance of compassion. Anything.

I see nothing but coldness.

"I've never been in trouble," I whisper. From the look on Natalie's face, nothing about me or my history matters right now.

I should have called my sister while I waited for Natalie. Brianna would know what to do.

But I don't know her phone number and, besides, my phone is in my locker. I memorized hundreds of drinks and I didn't bother to memorize my own sister's cell phone number.

Brianna can bail me out of jail. I'm going to jail.

I straighten in my chair and raise my chin. My uncle is an attorney. I can claim temporary insanity. Or permanent insanity. Whatever it takes.

Don't panic.

After making me sweat for what seems like an eternity, Natalie finally breaks the silence.

"Get your things out of your locker. Get out of here." She stands up straight. "Needless to say you're fired."

With disbelief, at being fired or not being hauled off to jail, I'm not sure, I stand up, feeling wobbly on my heels. I grasp the arm of the chair.

"You got lucky," Natalie says. "The girl's husband convinced her not to file charges."

"I don't even know her," I say as though that would work in my defense.

"All the more reason to not let her get to you. I suggest you find a different line of work."

I nod. I could not agree more.

I'm almost to the door when Natalie stops me.

"Lilah," she says.

"Yes?" I turn. I feel about two inches high and any kind word from Natalie. Any semblance of understanding. Would be a balm to my soul right now.

"Leave the dress."

I nod again and walk dazed back to the locker room.

I keep my eyes straight ahead. Fortunately I'm the only person back here. Everyone else is behind the bar or out on the floor working.

I never want to see any of these people again.

Grabbing my clothes out of my locker, I head to the

dressing room. My hands tremble as I slide the dress off over my head and put on a t-shirt in its place.

I manage to hold my emotions at bay as I scramble into my jeans. Slide my feet into my sneakers.

The woman, Bernice, could have pressed charges. I could have gone to jail.

If Trey said those things about me. About me being trash, then all I'd done is prove him right.

By the time I make it to my car, tucked away in the far corner of the parking lot, my hands are trembling so hard I can hardly wrap my fingers around my key fob. I close the door, and the quiet slams into me harder than any insult ever could.

In the darkness, I lean my forehead against the steering wheel. The scent of wine still lingers on my fingers. And then the tears come. Hot. Unstoppable. Until I'm shaking too hard to breathe.

CHAPTER
THREE

Lilah

"Drink this," Brianna shoves a mug of hot tea into my hands.

"I don't need tea," I say. "I need a whiskey."

I didn't call Brianna on the way home from work. She called me.

We have a circle of friends and family app on our phone that alerted her that I had left work early. I hadn't even considered that when I'd finally stopped crying long enough to drive out of the parking lot.

As such, she'd known something was wrong before I even answered the phone.

"I got fired," I'd told her.

"What happened?"

"I'll call you tomorrow. I just want to go home and go to bed."

Being the older sister that she is, she was waiting for me when I got home. I pretended to be annoyed, but the truth of it was I was happy to see her.

The first thing I'd done when I'd gotten home was to wash off my makeup. The streaks of dried mascara down my cheeks took a special solvent to get off.

And now Brianna wanted details. *I got fired* was not nearly enough to satisfy her.

"Drinking isn't going to solve anything. We need to figure out your next move."

Déjà vu. Almost unnaturally so.

It's been less than a month since Brianna and I'd had a similar conversation with our oldest sister Audrey.

Admittedly, Audrey's situation was a whole lot more dire than mine. Even though... if I'd gone to jail... my situation could have been pretty dire.

"You can't compare this to Audrey's situation," Brianna says, sitting on the arm of the couch, breathing in the steam from her own mug of tea.

"You're being a freaky mind-reader."

"Audrey's husband *died*. You getting fired doesn't even compare. You'll get another job."

"I don't want another job."

"Right. You do know you have to work, right? Our family is not independently wealthy."

I look up at her with something that tells her I think she's wrong.

"No," she says. "You cannot count Audrey's inheritance."

"Stop reading my mind!"

"It's hard to not read it when you just put your thoughts out there like that."

With a huff, I sip my hot tea. Even though I won't tell her, she's right. The hot tea is soothing.

Sliding next to me onto the old comfortable couch I'd gotten from my grandparents, she picks up a stack of index cards on my coffee table. It'd taken plain index cards and turned them into flashcards. The name of a drink on one side. The recipe on the other. Riffles through them.

"You spent so much time learning all these mixed drinks."

I shrug. "Yeah. Well." It stings. I can at least admit to myself that it stings. I could have been doing what I really love instead of memorizing drink recipes.

She hasn't even seen the cards on my nightstand. Different kinds of wines and what they go with.

"You're good at it, too."

"It's good brain exercise," I say.

"That's for sure." She puts my cards back down, slips off her shoes, and curls her feet beneath her.

"At least you still have your other job. Maybe you can pick up more hours there. You said they tip better anyway."

I'm already shaking my head. "No. I don't want anything to do with bartending."

"But..."

To make sure she understands just how much I mean it, I set my mug down and pick up the index cards. Well over four hundred of them. I take them over to the garbage can in my kitchen and dump them in.

"There," I say, wiping my hands together. "It's done."

"Maybe you should sleep on it."

"I'm going to sleep on it," I say. "But I won't change my mind."

"You might be overreacting."

I slide back into my spot on the couch and pick up my mug. "I almost got arrested. I don't think I'm over-reacting."

Brianna just shrugs.

"It's not what I want to do anyway," I say.

"I know," Brianna says with genuine compassion. "But sometimes it's like that."

"You don't understand." I murmur.

"I've known you your entire life," Brianna says. "I think I have a general idea of what makes you tick."

"Then you know I'm not cut out to work in the service industry."

She looks at me sideways. "You say. And yet out of the three of us, you're the most cut out for it."

"Well then, we must all be pretty bad off."

Brianna leans back and closes her eyes. She has brunette hair like Audrey. Long enough to curl softly around her shoulders, but she keeps it pulled back, leaving just a couple of strands loose around her face.

In addition to her usual vexed countenance, she looks tired.

"You didn't have to come over here tonight. I'll be okay."

"You're lucky she didn't press charges."

"I know. Can she change her mind? Come back and press charges anyway?"

"Yes. She has a two-year statute of limitations."

"Oh. My. God." I cover my face with my hands. "I have to sit on pins and needles for two years hoping she doesn't decide to press charges?"

"Yes."

"What do I do?" I turn to my sister." You're a paralegal. You must know some way to resolve this."

"I do," she says. "You wait,"

I close my eyes. My life just became a living hell.

"But... you can get a good attorney. They have footage showing that she provoked you. She followed you across the room and provoked you."

"Slander," I say. "She slandered me."

"What did she say exactly?"

"I don't want to talk about it." I sit back and hide my embarrassment behind my tea mug. How had Bernice known exactly what to say to me that would provoke me into a haze of anger?

Brianna gets up, goes to my kitchen, and comes back with a little notebook and a pen.

"What's this for?"

"Write it down. Write down everything you remember. Word for word. I know they have the video, but you need to put it down in your words. Include what you were feeling."

"I really don't want to relive it."

"Do it anyway. You asked what you could do. This is a way for you to preserve your memory. Don't look at me like that. I know you have a good memory, but two years is a long time. Memories fade."

"Fine." I set my mug aside and start writing. Once I start, I can't stop. The words just flow out of me onto the page.

Finished, I close the notebook. "What do I do with it?"

"Just keep it."

Great. A tangible reminder of what happened tonight.

The neighbors, a friendly couple in their thirties, pull into the lot, their headlights sweeping across the pavement before clicking off. They climb out of their car, their voices low and intimate, as they walk past, carrying the kind of easy warmth that only comes from years of being together.

"So you're quitting your other job?" Brianna asks.

"Yes."

"And then what? How are you going to pay your rent? What are you going to live off of?"

"I'll figure something out. Just not tonight."

"Like what?" Brianna challenges.

"I can go back to school. Get a master's degree."

"Good idea. I think that's a good idea. How much money do you have saved up?"

"Saved?" I look at her like she's lost her mind. "I can hardly pay my rent and my student loan payments."

"Lilah." Brianna gives me with that long-suffering look of hers.

"I can sell my paintings."

"Maybe. Didn't you try that once before?"

"Yes. But I didn't keep at it like I should have."

"You're back to the idea of being a starving artist."

"Maybe. Although I'm hoping to be something more than starving."

"Okay." Brianna takes a deep breath. Lets it out slowly. "I hate the idea, but you can come live with me."

"No. I don't think so." I pick up my mug of what is now lukewarm tea. "I have a better idea."

"That's not a good idea and you know it."

"You don't even know what my idea is."

"I know perfectly well what your idea is. You're thinking about going to live with Audrey."

I hate it when she does that. "Just until I figure things out."

"That's what they all say. I really think you need to reconsider."

"Fine," I say. "I'm going to sleep on it." I stand up. Stretch. "Right now would be good."

I want tonight to just go away. I want to wake up in the morning and find out it was all no more than a bad dream.

But unfortunately, my older sister has other ideas.

CHAPTER

FOUR

Lilah

"Lilah," Brianna says. "I know how much you love your art. Your painting and sketching." She looks around at the half dozen pieces of art I have displayed on my walls.

They're some of my favorites. But I can sell them if I have to. Anything to keep from going back to being a bartender.

The thought of walking back into a bar and working with the public makes me feel sick to my stomach.

"I know. It's not a real job." I sit back down and pull a throw around me.

Brianna is talking about my art now and it's like catnip to my soul. So I stay.

"Only a few people make a living at it. You can do it in your spare time. Like you've been doing."

What she really means is like I haven't been doing. Despite my good intentions, by the time I get home from working, I'm so exhausted, all I can do is fall into bed, then get up and do it all over again.

"We should call Audrey," Brianna says.

"No. We should not call Audrey." I don't want anyone else to know what happened tonight. I don't want anyone to know that I almost got myself arrested. I've never been so embarrassed in my entire life.

"You're going to have to tell her eventually," Brianna says.

"Why?"

"Don't ask stupid questions."

"Okay. I'll tell her I got fired. But not tonight."

"Okay," Brianna says. "Maybe tomorrow you'll wake up and decide that you can go back to the job you still have."

"The woman knew I'd dated Trey."

"Trey? That ass hat?"

"Yes." Brianna never liked Trey and obviously that has not changed.

"What did she say?"

I shake my head. I can't say it out loud. I'll never say it out loud. I'd rather die than tell anyone what Bernice said.

"It doesn't matter. But I'm never going to date again."

Brianna gives me one of her rare smiles. "You'll date again. You'll forget all about Trey. All about this night. And you'll date again."

"I don't think so. I've got two years for this to hang over my head. I can't be with someone and then suddenly get arrested. What would be the point? Just more embarrassment."

"Lilah. It's not the end of the world. Everything will look better in the morning. Whatever happens, you've got family support. You know that."

"I know." I blink back tears that threaten to spill over. I'd cried so much sitting in my car, I don't know where I could possibly have more, but here they are, welling in my eyes.

Maybe it's a sign to do what I've been thinking about.

"Will you help me pack?" I blurt.

"What?"

"Will you help me pack up this place?" I straighten, gesturing around my little one-bedroom apartment. "I've been thinking about moving and now seems like a good time to do it. My lease is out. I'm running month-to-month."

"Okay. I've got the day off tomorrow." She runs a hand over the arm of my couch. "If you're moving in with me, we'll need to sell your furniture."

"I was thinking I could put it in storage."

"A complete waste of money. By the time you're ready

to move out and get your own place again, you'll want new furniture."

I run a hand over the old threadbare linen-weave couch. "Okay. I'll sell it."

I'll sell my furniture, but I don't know that I'm moving in with Brianna.

Brianna lives in Houston and apparently one person too many recognizes me in Houston.

It's time for me to get away from here.

I've overstayed my welcome.

CHAPTER
FIVE

Wyatt Winslow

I PROP A LOG ON A STUMP, lift my axe, and drop it down, splitting the log into two perfect pieces. The two pieces fall with a crash on either side of the stump.

I balance one of them on the stump and repeat the process.

We have commercial grade log splitters. Kindling splitters. Wood chippers. Everything a man could possibly need to make his own firewood without wielding an axe.

But, what can I say, I like chopping firewood by hand.

There's something inherently satisfying about the process.

When I was no more than a boy, my grandfather on the Winslow side taught me how to chop down trees, how to chop them into firewood, and how to lay a perfect fire.

My grandparents on our mother's side taught me to appreciate the arts. I'd spent two summers in Boston with them, rotating summers with my two older brothers.

My oldest brother, Bradley learned how to cook during his summer rotation. Since I didn't take to the kitchen, they took me to museums and art galleries.

I discovered I have a special affinity for the classics like Monet and van Gogh. Not something I would ever tell my brothers. They would never let me live it down.

My brothers and I, the Winslow boys, are known around the little town of Whiskey Springs, Colorado for being rugged, manly men. We own and operate our family business Timber Ridge Cabins and Timber Company.

As of last count, we have thirty-seven cabins. One of those cabins, I claimed for myself. My two brothers each claimed one for themselves, too. The other thirty-four are for tourists. We're always buying and selling cabins, though, so that number is fluid.

The cabin I'm living in right now, in fact, is a renovation project. Once I have it renovated, I'll be moving out and it'll go into the rental column. I'm taking my time on it, though, because I like the location. It sits right next to the rushing Whiskey Springs river and there's nothing like falling asleep with the sound of the river right outside my window.

Our busiest seasons are summer, of course, and oddly enough Christmas. People flock to Whiskey Springs for the trails and quiet serenity in the summers and the town's holiday festivities in December.

Our grandpa was a descendant of one of the first settlers of Whiskey Springs and he'd turned out to be a real estate mogul in his own right. He'd started the whole thing that got us where we are today.

I set the axe down as my brother drives up in his black Ford F-150 pickup truck. All three of us drive them, new ones, and our father drives an older model. Not only are they convenient for hauling everything from firewood to appliances, it makes us easy to recognize without putting billboards on the sides of our trucks. No one wants to drive around in a billboard.

Bradley gets out, his big gangly black lab named Biscuit climbing out with him and running in my direction.

Seeing me, Bradley follows along behind the dog.

Biscuit puts his feet up on either one of my shoulders and licks me in the face. He's big as a horse and sweet as a kitten.

"Yeah. I'm happy to see you, too."

"That dog has absolutely no manners."

"Wouldn't be Biscuit if he had any manners." I lift the dog's paws off my shoulders and drop them to the ground.

Wiggling all over, his tongue hanging out in unadulterated bliss, the dog runs circles around both of us.

"Wish I had some of that energy," Bradley says.

"You look troubled."

"Those cameras we installed around Audrey's house might have been for nothing."

"Why do you say that?" I pick up my fallen logs, stacking them off to the side. Bradley helps.

Bradley and I had spent most of yesterday installing a security system of cameras around Audrey's house. I learned to install security cameras by helping out a friend and turns out I'm pretty good at it. Gives me a little side hustle.

"Somebody left a note in her book."

"Her book?"

"Yeah. Some novel she's reading. Left it right there like a bookmark."

"We just put those cameras up yesterday. Maybe they left the note before that."

This is the third time someone left threatening notes for her. The first two were left on the front porch while Bradley and Audrey were inside. Dropped off right under their noses.

"Maybe." Bradley straightens. Looks off into the distance toward nothing in particular.

"But…"

"But I don't think so. She reads every night. She would have noticed."

"Maybe she missed a night."

"Yeah. Maybe. Anyway, her sister is coming in this morning. You want to grab some lunch?"

"I'm always up for some lunch. The Hungry Biscuit?"

"Sure. You drive."

"What's wrong with you? You always drive."

"Trouble sleeping. Worrying about those stupid notes."

I grab my jacket and throw it over my shoulder. "You should run for sheriff."

"Why would I do that?"

We climb into my truck and I start the motor.

"Why not? You'd do better than that yahoo we got in there now."

"And who would manage all the renovations we've got going on?"

I put the truck in reverse. "You talking about the Bentley cabin? That's almost finished."

"Hardly."

"Added something else?"

"Yeah. I decided to add on a back deck."

"You do know that I'm quite capable of doing that, right?"

"Figured you'd help out."

I turn onto the highway and we head toward Whiskey Springs.

Our parents live in the city limits of Whiskey Springs, but us three brothers live out in the secluded cabins.

Bradley lives further out than any of us. He lives up the mountain meaning near the end of a deserted dirt road. The only person who lives further up his road is Audrey living in the Albright place.

Audrey Sinclair, from Houston, had inherited the Albright place after her husband was killed in a private plane crash a few weeks ago.

She'd no more than moved out here when she started getting threatening notes. All anonymous. Somebody claiming she doesn't belong in the house.

We pull up to the Hungry Biscuit, a growing local chain, claiming to have the best burgers and fries, a senti-ment I don't disagree with, to find it crowded.

I park across the street and we walk over. Get in line.

"You got time to take a load of firewood out to Audrey's this afternoon?"

"I just took her firewood."

"I don't mean a cord. Just top her off. And while you're there see if three cameras are enough to line the road up to her place."

"Why didn't you just ask me to check about the cameras?"

"Two birds," he says sheepishly.

I study him while he gives his name to the hostess. We step back to wait outside.

The air is brisk, even for June. One thing I love about Whiskey Springs is that it rarely gets hot even in the heart of summer.

"I know what you're up to."

"Not up to anything," he says too quickly.

"You just want me to meet her sister. And. You haven't even met her yet."

"Hey." Bradley holds up his hands. "You told me you wanted to meet Audrey's sisters. Wasn't my idea."

"I think you should meet her first."

"Chicken. She's Audrey's sister. She can't help but be anything but hot."

"There's more to a girl than looking hot," I say with a grumble.

"Speaking of the devil," Bradley says. "There's Sheriff Morgan."

I look up just in time to see the sheriff step up to the hostess's stand.

"Ass hat," I mutter under my breath.

Bradley looks over at me. "What is it you dislike so much about him?"

"Just something about him. Can't explain it."

"Mr. Winslow."

"Our table's ready."

"Good.

Walking inside and following the hostess to our table, Bradley speaks to the sheriff. I pretend I don't see him standing there.

I don't know what it is. Something about him just rubs me the wrong way.

CHAPTER
SIX

Lilah

I WAKE UP COMPLETELY DISORIENTED.

Soft sunlight spills across my face, but the air is unusually chilly. A different kind of chilly than the usual coolness from the air conditioner.

Then the pieces start to come together along with the sounds floating in through the window cracked just enough to let in some fresh air. Sounds of the river flowing easily within walking distance and birds singing their morning song in the limbs of the fragrant blue spruce trees damp with morning dew.

Needless to say, I'm not in my apartment in Houston

and I'm not in one of the dingy motels I'd spent the night in getting here.

I'm at my sister's new home. The Albright house just outside of Whiskey Springs. In the Rocky Mountains of Colorado.

The home she inherited from her late husband's grandfather.

The inheritance came with conditions. Significant conditions.

She has to live in the house and she can't sell it.

But. It also comes with perks.

Lots of perks.

All expenses paid. And she gets a substantial annual stipend gifted to her. One million dollars.

One million dollars at the beginning of every year. The first deposit hit her account the minute she sighed the papers.

Brianna had been the most skeptical of all. I had been the one who was most in favor of it.

It had been my opinion that Audrey had to do it. She had to move here. As far as I could see, she didn't really have a choice.

And now she has a new boyfriend.

The three of us had gone into town for pizza last night.

His name is Bradley Winslow. The oldest son of an influential family in town.

They own dozens of cabins around the town, mostly

in the outlying areas. They also own a lucrative timber company, supplying firewood to the county. Apparently they plant as many trees as they cut down. It's admirable how they're protecting the environment while making a good living.

I can tell by the way Bradley looks at my sister that he likes her.

She's worried that it's too soon to be interested in anyone after losing her husband.

I tried to assure her that there are no rules.

Seeing the way they look at each other says everything to me.

If she wants to be with Bradley Winslow, then nobody says they shouldn't be together. Not in my book.

I stretch and think about my day stretching ahead. No bartending jobs to go to.

My sister, Brianna, is right. I have to have income to live. I know I'll have to look for a job. But for now... for today at least... I can take a deep breath and not worry about having to go to work.

I feel rested enough to unload my paints and canvases from the car. I certainly didn't feel like it yesterday. I've never driven this far and certainly not by myself. Driving across Houston from downtown to Katy doesn't count, even though no one can say it's not a long way.

It was a very very long drive from Houston to Whiskey Springs and I'm thinking I'm not going to do it again.

If I need to go back to Houston, I'll save up my money and get an airplane ticket.

Putting my feet on the cold floor, I hurry across to the bathroom.

Cold floors in June. Interesting.

I've never cared much for the heat that comes with living in Houston. Always just saw it as part of the way things were.

Born and bred in the south. It's just the way things are.

But now that I'm here, I'm seeing that there are other ways to live.

I dig my slippers out of my suitcase and slide a sweater on over my pajamas.

It's early, but I'm ready to locate the coffee machine and start my day.

The first day of my new life.

CHAPTER
SEVEN

Wyatt

"Wʜᴀᴛ ᴛʜᴇ——?"

I roll over and look at the digital clock glowing brightly on my nightstand.

Seven thirty in the morning.

Who the hell is knocking on my door at seven thirty in the morning on a Saturday morning?

I slide out of bed, pull on a pair of jeans and a flannel shirt before making my bleary-eyed way out of the bedroom and across the living room to the door.

I open the door to find my brother Bradley standing there holding two coffee cups. He's grinning like a loon.

I take one of the coffee cups, slam the door in his face, and turn around.

It doesn't stop him. He just opens up the door and walks right in like he owns the place.

"You're welcome," Bradley says.

My only answer is to take a sip of coffee. "To what do I owe the pleasure of this early morning wake-up call?"

"Just wanted to repay the thanks the couple in the Smith cabin called and woke me up with."

"The Smith cabin. Nice couple. What did they want?"

"They just wanted to let us know how grateful they are that you came out on a Friday night and fixed their shower."

"Wasn't a problem," I say, flopping down on my couch. "Where's the dog?"

"I left Biscuit at Audrey's."

"So really. Why are you here so early?"

"Had to run into town and while I was there I bought coffee."

"Didn't have to do that."

"I owed it to you."

"For what?"

"For thinking you'd fabricated an excuse for not going out for pizza with us last night."

I run a hand through my hair and look at my brother. "Why would I do that?"

He sits on the arm of the couch and tips his coffee cup back for a sip. "Can't imagine why."

"So," I say. "What's the verdict?"

"You'll like her."

"The sister."

"Her name is Lilah."

"You like her," I say, still trying to get my brain to wake up and fighting the irritation at having my plans to sleep half the day away thwarted so rudely.

"I like her as Audrey's sister. Yes." Bradley stretches out his legs. "I think you'll like her."

"Not interested."

"Wait a minute." Bradley sits forward and looks at me. "When you met Audrey, you were all for meeting her sister."

"That was before you went and fell in love with Audrey."

Bradley looks at me like I've lost my mind.

"I don't know why you'd say that."

"You don't even know it. It's written all over your face."

He doesn't say anything for a minute. Someone on a motorcycle drives past. A guest staying at the cabin up the road.

"That has nothing to do with you and Lilah," he says finally.

"It actually has a lot to do with it."

"Please explain."

"It seems self-explanatory enough to me," I say,

running a hand over my face. Now that I'm up, I need to shave. "If you and Audrey are going to get married—"

"I didn't say anything about getting married."

"Okay. If there is any possibility that you and Audrey MIGHT get married, I don't want to risk getting involved with the sister. It could make family gatherings… uncomfortable."

He swirls his coffee cup. "I see your point," he says. "And you could be right."

"I'm right."

"But there's also the possibility that you could like her."

"You know I don't do long-term commitments."

"You could change your mind," Bradley says.

"Right." I can see where he might think that, but there is no way in hell I'm going to change my mind.

It's just not going to happen.

"By the way," Bradley says. "The wireless cameras came in. They're out in the truck. Think you can go out to Audrey's house with me today and put them up?"

"I should have known you wanted something. You could have led with that."

"And where would the fun be in that?" Bradley asks.

Brothers. Can't live with them. Can't live without them.

EIGHT

Lilah

"Good morning," I say, finding Audrey in the kitchen, before I see that she's feeding that humongous horse of a dog they call Biscuit.

Seeing me, Biscuit runs over and puts his head beneath my hand. I take a step back. Wary of this giant dog. And yet he seems so friendly.

"He just wants you to pet him," Audrey says. "He won't hurt you."

"So you say."

"Biscuit." Audrey pats her leg. "Come here."

The dog goes back to Audrey and starts eating the food she puts down for him. "You want coffee?" she asks.

"Please. Where's Bradley?"

"Work. I guess." She gets two mugs down and starts making coffee. "He doesn't exactly actually live here."

"Not exactly." I take the cup of coffee she hands me. "This is good. Almost like designer."

"It is designer. Homemade designer."

"I'm a little surprised you know how to work that fancy machine."

She shrugs. "Bradley showed me. It's easy." She finishes making her own cup of coffee and looks at me. "Want to sit on the deck?"

"Okay. But it might be too cold."

"You get used to it. Besides. The sun is warm. It's a nice combination. Warm sun and cool breeze."

As she opens the back door, Biscuit runs out past us.

As we step outside behind him, Audrey hesitates, looking around.

"So," I say, sitting down on one of the chairs at the little outdoor table. "Bradley lives here, but he doesn't *live* here. Sounds a little confusing to me."

"He's staying here. To keep me safe."

"What's he doing?" I ask, nodding toward the dog walking around the perimeter of the yard, staying just on this side the tree line.

"He's just making his rounds. Making sure everything is as it should be."

"So he's like a guard dog."

"He's a very good guard dog. He hears things before we do."

I shiver involuntarily. "How do you stand it? Always being on alert?"

"Stubborn?"

"It's a new look for you," I say. "It's good." I warm my hands on the mug.

"I like it here."

"Hmm."

"Hmm what?"

"Nothing. I just wonder how much you liking it here has to do with Bradley."

"I liked it here before I met him," she says.

I narrow my eyes at her. "And that was all of what? Five minutes?"

"Maybe," she says with a little smile.

"It's good to see you smiling again."

"It's good to have something to smile about."

"How are you doing? With the whole Thomas thing?"

"I'm okay," she says, but the smile isn't there anymore. "There was so much all at once. Him dying in the plane crash. Finding out he had a child with someone else and he'd never even told me. His insurance going to the baby and the mother."

"It's a lot," I say, rather wishing I hadn't brought it up. "But you came out better than you would have with the insurance. Getting money in your account every year."

"That's true."

"Does Bradley know about that?"

"I didn't tell him."

I watch Biscuit dig a hole in the ground, sending dirt and foliage scattering, like he suddenly found the secret treasure he was searching for.

"I know it's not my business, but..." I say.

"But you're going to tell me anyway."

"I can wait. It's not important."

"Just tell me already."

"If you and Bradley do happen to get serious... Not saying you will. I know he's just *staying* here to protect you. But if you do get serious and he does move in for real, don't you think you should tell him?"

"Because it's like Thomas keeping secrets from me." She sits back and sighs. "I didn't think of it like that. I guess I'm still getting used to the idea of getting the money. I check my account every day to see if it's still there."

I smile. "It's not going anywhere."

And if my gut sense is right, neither is Bradley.

CHAPTER
NINE

Wyatt

As we planned ahead of time, Bradley drove ahead to check on Audrey.

If ever there was a man smitten, it's my dear heartsick brother.

I feel fortunate I have never had the misfortune to suffer such a state. He can't go two seconds without saying something about her and I feel certain she's front and center in his thoughts constantly.

While he drives on up to her house, the house I still think of and probably always will, as the Albright house, I stop a few yards out and pull over onto the side of the road and get out.

Pulling over is just a habit. Not a necessity out here. The one-lane dirt road ends at Audrey's house.

I grab one of the camouflage painted security camera boxes and, tucking it under my arm, leave the road to look for areas a person might do just what I'm doing. Get out of their vehicle and walk up to the house.

Whoever has been leaving the threatening notes on Audrey's doorstep needs to be stopped. Has to be stopped. Before they escalate into doing something more serious.

I walk along what looks like an elk trail, circling around toward the back of the house.

I hear the rushing water of the river before I see it.

Personally, I like the way my little cabin sits right on the riverbank. So far, it's never flooded, but that's always a possibility. Up here, the house is high enough, it's not going to flood. Not possible unless water starts running uphill.

I've been out here walking before. I don't even remember why. I do remember that the old man Albright was alive at the time.

Actually there's a trail, or used to be, from the Albright place to the cabin Bradley is currently living in. No one uses it. I guess it's easier to just drive.

It's as pretty up here as I remember. A clear view of the snow-capped mountains across the valley. A meadow sweeping down from the back deck of the house to the river.

This is the perfect elevation. Below tree line. High enough that trees flourish. Aspens. Maples. Fragrant blue spruce trees.

The meadow is dotted with blue and white flowers waving in the breeze. Little sparrows fluttering among them as well as bees buzzing from flower to flower.

When I see her, I stop in my tracks.

A slim, young lady. Light brown hair with streaks of blonde fluttering about her shoulders. She'd pulled it back, but the wind has tugged strands loose that she shoves back with her wrist.

She's wearing a light green printed full skirt that bellows in the breeze and a chunky emerald green wool sweater. A combination that works for her. A hat she seems to have forgotten she was wearing hangs down her back, tied at her neck in a bow.

She stands in front of a painter's easel, a paint brush in her left hand, and a wooden paint palette in her right hand.

I can't see what she's painting and frankly I don't care. She could be painting nothing but circles and I would find it beautiful.

Just as I've never seen anyone as beautiful as she is. Her features are delicate. Like I would imagine a fairy princess would look.

I don't know how long I stand there, just taking her in.

I could look at her, simply look at her, for hours. Mesmerized. Just mesmerized.

She doesn't see me. She's completely focused on what she's painting.

Somewhere in the back of my mind, it registers with me that this is all the more reason to have security cameras out here.

I don't know who she is. Where she came from. What her name is.

All I know is that I have fallen utterly and completely head over heels in love.

Lilah

THE WIND BLOWS SOFTLY TOSSING the hair I'd pulled back across my face. The hat I'd borrowed from Audrey slides off my head, hanging against my back, secured only by a bow around my neck.

My sister had been right. The warmth of the sun offsets the chilliness of the breeze coming off the river.

The water, rushing over boulders of all sizes, rumbles along the river, sending the occasional water spray in my direction. But the air is so dry, it dries almost immediately.

The paintbrush feels a little rusty in my hand at first,

but it only take a few streaks on the canvas to have me getting back in the groove.

The scent of the paints in my palette are better than the most expensive perfume. There's nothing I love more than the feel of a brush in my hands and the scent of fresh paint on a canvas.

I heard a truck pull up to the house. I'm not far. I'm not brave enough to venture out of earshot of the house. Hear Biscuit bark as Bradley gets out of his truck and gives him a treat.

I don't see the matching black truck stop a ways down the road. Not at first, anyway.

When I see the man standing at the edge of the forest, watching me, I sense no danger. None.

Even less when I spot his black truck, exactly like Bradley's parked not too far away.

It doesn't take much for me to put it all together. Maybe all those brain exercises, memorizing mixed drinks, was paying off.

This has to be Wyatt Winslow, Bradley's brother. He has a similar look, except that Wyatt looks more rugged, like he belongs outdoors.

I let him watch me paint. Mostly because I don't want to stop. I've been looking forward to getting out here, setting the artist trapped inside me free.

Finally, after what could have been two minutes, probably closer to five, I look up and meet his gaze.

He looks a little startled. As though he didn't expect me to see him standing there.

I would've had to be blind not to see him. Not so much because he stands out. On the contrary, he blends in with the terrain with his brown flannel shirt and jeans. He's wearing a baseball cap over short, dark hair.

I would've had to be blind not to see him simply because of the way he watches me. As though he's never seen an artist at work.

"Would you like to see it?" I ask him. "The painting. Would you like to see it?"

"Sure."

"Well. You have to come over here."

He seems to come out of his daze and walk over to me.

He stops right in front of me, his eyes never leaving mine. "It's beautiful."

I smile. "You haven't even looked at it yet."

"I don't have to see it to know. I already know it's lovely."

I shrug and dab my paint brush into a mix of white and blue, making an even lighter blue. One that matches the color of his eyes.

I touch the paint lightly to the canvas, turning a dot of paint into the image of a pale blue wildflower.

"You make it look so easy," he says.

I glance up. He's watching me paint now.

"Do you paint?" I ask.

"No. But I appreciate art. And you have talent."

"You know art?"

"I spent a fair amount of time in the Museum of Fine Arts in Boston."

"I'm impressed." I dab more flowers onto the page, mostly because he seems to like them. "And surprised."

He looks back at me now, with a little smile on his lips. "You don't expect to meet anyone out here who appreciates art."

"I rarely meet anyone anywhere who appreciates art."

"I find that very sad."

"It is sad."

"You must be Wyatt," I say, adding some green paint to my brush.

"And you must be Lilah."

"Impressed and surprised once more."

"My brother is in love with your sister and your name has come up."

"I knew she was wrong," I say, stepping back to study my canvas.

"Who was wrong about what?"

"Audrey. She thinks Bradley is just here temporarily. To protect her."

"Sometimes it takes a minute to figure those things out."

"Sometimes," I say, meeting his gaze again.

"Sometimes not."

Something in those blue eyes tug at me and tell me we aren't talking about our siblings any more.

"What's that?" I ask. "Under your arm."

"What?" He seems to have forgotten he was holding something. He pulls it out and glances at it. "Security camera to keep you safe."

"Are you supposed to be installing it?" I glance past him. "Bradley's on his way out here with a ladder."

"Right. Yes." He doesn't look away. "Will you have dinner with me? Tonight?"

"Okay," I say, more than little amused.

"And tomorrow night?"

"I don't know. Aren't we supposed to see how tonight goes?"

"Who makes these rules?"

"I don't know."

"Wyatt," Bradley calls. "Where do you want me to put the ladder?"

"I have to go. I'll pick you up at six."

As he walks away to join his brother, I remember with a bit of annoyance at myself that it was only days ago that I vowed to myself to never date again.

CHAPTER
ELEVEN

Wyatt

"Wyatt," Bradley says. "What's wrong with you?"

"Nothing." I tear my gaze away from Lilah and focus my attention on the hole I'm drilling in a maple tree.

"Watch what you're doing. You're going to fall off the ladder and break your fool neck."

"Hand me that camera," I say, purposely keeping my gaze off of Lilah. For two seconds. Just to show Bradley that I can.

With the camera installed, I look back over at Lilah. She's folding up her easel, getting ready to go inside. Disappointment slides through me, settling in my veins.

I climb down the ladder and watch her easily gather up her things and head back to the house.

"Maybe you could be a little more obvious," Bradley says.

"Maybe."

Once she's inside, I turn back to Bradley.

"You need to decide what you're going to do about Audrey."

"Why? Audrey is mine."

"No question there. You just need to decide what you're going to do."

"Why is that?"

"Because I'm going to marry Lilah."

"What's wrong with you? You met her two seconds ago."

"When you know, you know."

"Come on," Bradley says. "Where do we need to put the next camera?"

"On the road," I say. "To catch anyone driving up."

"I thought that's what we were going to do anyway."

"Never said it wasn't."

Biscuit comes running toward us at a gallop. He must have slipped out past Lilah.

He runs circles around us before sitting in front of Bradley to bark for a treat.

"Got him trained," I say.

"The treats were Audrey's idea."

"Biscuit isn't complaining. Put the ladder on this tree

over here. We'll shoot it right down the road. Catch them coming around the big curve."

Bradley props the ladder against the tree as instructed. "So when is the wedding?"

"We're not there yet." Pull the next camera out of its box. "She doesn't know about it yet."

"I see. She doesn't know that she's marrying you."

I climb up three rungs. Look down at him. "Well. No. We just met."

Bradley bursts out laughing. "Something is seriously wrong with you."

"Yeah. Well. At least I know what I want when I see it."

"Didn't say I don't know what I want. But." He hands me the drill. "As you oldest brother, I need to caution you about something."

"What's that?" I turn on the drill. Make a small hole in the tree.

"Girls don't like being told what they're going to do."

"Bro. Thanks for the brotherly advice. But I think I've got this."

"Okay." Bradley holds up his hands. "I did my job. I told you."

"They don't like to be left waiting either," I say under my breath.

"It's only been a couple of weeks," Bradley says.

"Seriously? It's creepy when you do that."

"I might be older than you are, but I'm not deaf."

I whistle as I attach the camera to the tree, pleased with the way it blends in among the leaves. "You'll need to keep an eye on this one. Make sure the leaves don't obstruct the view."

And while I'm at it, maybe I'll download the app onto my phone so I can get alerts, too. Can't have too many of us watching after our girls.

CHAPTER

TWELVE

Lilah

AFTER STOWING my paints supplies and easel away in my room, I wash the paint from my hands and take a peek into my closet.

My sister and Bradley had gutted it, pulling out any rods and shelves, then sheetrocking the walls. A blank slate, it smells like fresh paint.

Audrey's letting me have input on how I want to design it.

I like this old house. With updates, it's as good as new. I especially like all the windows, even though Audrey has ordered shades to cover them at night.

She doesn't feel safe having the windows uncovered in light of someone leaving threatening notes on the front porch.

I don't blame her. And now that I'm here, I have little doubt that whoever is trying run her off will be trying to run me off, too.

I'm not a threat though. Not like Audrey. The house is in Audrey's name and she's the one getting the inheritance trust money.

If I stay here, I'll need to find a way to pull my weight. I've got some ideas about how to sell my paintings online. Copies of them anyway. I'll sell the originals, too, but that's less likely to happen.

I have to be realistic. I'm thinking I can paint one new painting every day, then spent the rest of my work day posting things online.

I find my sister in her bedroom, bent over a pad of graph paper.

"Well," I say, sitting on her bed. "That was interesting."

"What? Your painting session?" She looks up.

"No. The painting was fine."

Audrey sets her pad of paper aside. "What was more interesting than painting?"

"Wyatt Winslow."

"You met Wyatt? Bradley said he was out looking for somewhere to... oh... You met Wyatt."

"Yes." I bite my lip to keep from smiling.

"Was he nice to you?"

I lay back on the bed and stare up at the ceiling. "Of course." I look over at my sister. "Why wouldn't he be?"

"Just asking." She picks up her graph paper. Studies it. "I already figured out what to do with my closet."

"Already? How? You just got here."

"It's not that hard."

She blows out a breath. "I just want it to be perfect, you know?"

"Nothing's ever perfect. Just build it. Then if you don't like it, you can tear it out and start over. It's not like you don't have enough money."

"You're probably right."

She turns to a fresh page of graph paper. "How are we doing your closet?"

Shelves down one side. Two rows of hanging rods on the other. The top row all the way across. The bottom row only halfway across to leave room for dresses and skirts."

Audrey looks up at me. "It's so simple. What about drawers?"

"I've got a dresser in my room."

"You do, don't you?" She glances around. "I could get a dresser."

"You should get a dresser. Get something nice and sturdy. Good quality."

"I can see that."

"We can drive into Denver. Look around. We need new furniture."

"We. You've decided to move in?"

"I'm still thinking about it." I've already pretty much decided I am, but I'm not ready to tell her that. Not when I made that decision before I left Houston.

"So what did you think about Wyatt?"

"Wyatt is... not what I expected."

"More rugged than Bradley."

"Exactly. But..."

"But...?"

"I don't know. He's kind of sweet."

"Wyatt?"

"Are we talking about the same Wyatt?"

"I sure hope so." I lean up on one elbow. "Because we're going out tonight."

CHAPTER

THIRTEEN

Bradley

AFTER SUCCESSFULLY MOUNTING the security cameras out at Audrey's house, I stop by my parents' house to wash my truck.

By the time I get the truck washed, it's time for me to head back to my cabin. Take a shower and get dressed for my date with Lilah.

After taking a shower and shaving, I put on a pair of black dress pants, a white button-down shirt, and a leather jacket. With Lilah being from the city, I'm thinking she'll be impressed with the look. I even put on my good lace-up leather shoes.

I'm feeling a little bit overdressed, but I don't want her to think that just because I live in a small town I don't know how to clean myself up.

I leave early to give myself time to stop by the General Store to see if they happen to have any fresh flowers.

"What can I get for you?" John, the owner of the General Store asks as I walk toward the checkout counter.

The General Store has just about anything anyone could want. John carries everything from milk to t-shirts to firewood.

"Got any fresh flowers?" I ask.

"No. But it looks like I'm going to have to start carrying them. People keep asking me for them."

"That's too bad." Apparently he does not carry *everything* a person could want.

"You got a date?"

"Yes. I do, as a matter of fact."

"Let me guess. The Sinclair sister. The one that just got here."

"Does everyone know everything?"

"Pretty much. You're from here. You know everybody knows everybody else's business."

"How could you possibly know that?"

"I didn't. I heard she was coming into town and I guessed. Guessed right, too, didn't I?" He grins smugly.

"I guess you did. Think they have any flowers up at the lodge?"

"Nah. They don't have flowers either. Fresh flowers

are a big investment. I could have them delivered in, then go weeks without someone asking for flowers."

"Why doesn't someone put up a greenhouse? Keep flowers on hand all year round?"

John looks at me as though I've just said either the stupidest thing or the most brilliant thing he's ever heard.

Apparently the most brilliant. He points a finger at me. "That's what my wife needs. She's been needing something to occupy her time since she retired from teaching."

"Well then. There you go."

"Let me think on it. You up for building it?"

"Sure. I can build it. Now I just need a bouquet of flowers. For tonight."

"Hold on." He picks up his phone. Starts typing.

I lean against the counter and flip through the pages of a scenic calendar of the Rocky Mountains he has for sale.

He must have been texting because I hear a response come back.

"If you don't mind fresh picked flowers, the wife has some roses growing in our backyard. Says you're welcome to cut a dozen."

"Actually. If she has roses, all I need is one."

"Head on over there. Pick one out. I'll call you about that greenhouse."

"You're one of the good ones, John."

"Just don't tell the wife about the greenhouse yet. I want to talk to her first."

"I won't say a word."

I check my watch as I head out. I have just enough time to run over and get a rose from John's backyard, then drive up to the Albright house. If I hurry.

Maybe it will pay off in the long run. If John builds that greenhouse so we always have fresh flowers. But in the short term, I can't be late for my date.

FOURTEEN

Lilah

"I KNEW it was too good to be true," I say coming downstairs.

"What's too good to be true?" Audrey asks from where she's sitting with Bradley in front of the fireplace with the roaring fire.

On second thought, I decide not to voice my disappointment in front of Wyatt's brother. "Nothing. Who's that?" There's a black cat sitting on the far end of the sectional, away from them.

"This is Blackie," Audrey says. "Bradley just brought him home from the vet in Boulder."

"Is he okay?"

"He was just getting checked out. The doc says he's in good health. Had to buy special senior cat food for him though."

I sit down next to the cat. He's a solid black cat with thick short hair.

"Hi Blackie," I say, sitting next to him. He takes a tentative step, then climbs into my lap.

"It's a good thing I'm wearing a black dress." Blackie puts his front feet on my shoulders and rubs his face against my chin.

"He likes her," Audrey says. "He acted afraid of us."

"It's because you two smell like dog." The dog in question is curled up in front of the fireplace sleeping. "Have they met?"

"Sort of," Audrey says glancing at Bradley.

"They acted like they didn't see each other."

"That's kind of odd." Blackie sits down in my lap and purrs. I glance at my watch.

It's four minutes until six. If Wyatt doesn't show up in four minutes, I'm going back upstairs and get ready for bed.

I'm not supposed to be dating anyway. Not after what happened with Trey. Not with the cloud of being arrested hanging over my head for the next two years.

It'd for the best if he didn't show up.

"How long is Blackie staying?" I ask.

"Until Claire gets out of jail."

I wince. "Right. But you don't think Claire's the one who left the notes."

"I know she's not. She couldn't possibly be. She was in the hospital when the second note was left."

"Why would she get arrested then?"

"That's what we can't figure out," Bradley says. "The sheriff says her prints were all over the notes."

"Maybe someone set her up." I rub Blackie under the chin and he purrs even louder.

Audrey and Bradley look at each other again. They're already acting like a couple. I'm both surprised and pleased at how my sister is doing.

I had expected her to still be grieving and I'm sure she has a lot going on in her head, but by all outward appearances, she appears to be doing remarkably well.

I haven't really talked to her about it, not seriously. And I don't want to open up any wounds she's healing on her own.

Sometimes things are best left alone.

Two minutes. Wyatt has two minutes to get here.

"Well," I say to the cat in my lap. "I'm going to head upstairs. Get ready for bed."

"Don't you have a date?" Audrey asks.

"He's not here." I shrug. "So I guess not."

"He'll be here," Bradley says. "If he says he'll be here, he'll be here."

"Maybe I misunderstood."

"I don't think so." Bradley glances at his watch.

That's when I hear the truck drive up and stop outside. One minute. Wyatt made it with one minute to spare.

"I'll get it," Bradley says. "You're occupied."

"Blackie. I'm pleased to meet you, too. But I have to get up now."

"Come on, Blackie." Audrey pulls Blackie out of my lap, but he won't let her hold him. When I stand up, Blackie sits down in my spot.

"I don't think she likes the smell of Biscuit."

"Maybe. She'll have to get used to it."

"Do I have cat hair on me?" I ask.

"No," Audrey says, sweeping a hand down my sleeves to be sure. "You're good."

"Okay." I give her a smile. "Time for me to go then."

"Have fun."

"Thanks," I say, turning around.

I blink.

The man standing next to Bradley looks like a completely different man from the man I'd seen by the river.

I blink again.

Wyatt Winslow is looking at me with a little sideways grin that I know deep in my gut is going to be my undoing.

He doesn't fit any molds that I carry in my head.

Not a city guy, too soft to work with his hands.

Not the lumberjack he'd looked like when I'd first seen him.

No. The Wyatt Winslow standing in my sister's living room is someone entirely different. Someone I don't quite have a readymade spot for in my head.

"Hi," he says, taking a step forward.

"Hi. I didn't think—" I was going to say something about him not making it on time, but the words drift away, forgotten, when he pulls a single red, dewy rose from behind his back and holds it out to me.

We walk toward each other, both moving at the same time. I take the rose from his hand, pressing the rose's dewy softness against my cheek.

"It smells fresh. Like outside."

"It's fresh from the garden," he says.

"Really?" It looks like it's fresh from the garden. A little bit wild. Not like the perfect roses that come from the flower shops.

In that way, it reminds me of Wyatt.

FIFTEEN

Wyatt

BRADLEY AND AUDREY fade into the background the moment I see Lilah.

I honestly don't know if they're even in the same room with us.

All I can see is Lilah.

She's wearing a little black dress that skims her slim body in all the right places. Her blondish hair is swept over shoulder. Straight and smooth with just a hint of curl at the ends.

I don't know much about women's hairstyles, but it looks like maybe she spent some time on it.

Something glimmers on her eyelids and her lips are glossy. A different, more polished look than she'd worn when I'd met her.

I'm instantly thankful I'd worn something worthy of being seen with her. And I log the information. Lilah is not the kind of girl a guy wears jeans on a date with. She's the kind of girl a guy would pull out the tux on special occasions. In fact, a tux would not have me overdressed tonight. I guess I unconsciously knew that when she wore a skirt outside to paint.

But it's her green eyes beneath dark lashes that pull me in and suck me right under.

I'm a man lost at sea. There's no finding my way back and I wouldn't want to if I could.

"I should probably put this in water," she says, her gaze locked onto mine.

"Probably." But neither one of us moves.

"I'll just bring it," she decides.

"Okay." I glance over to where Bradley and Audrey are sitting on the sofa pretending not to watch us. "Lock us out," I say to Bradley. "Ready?" I ask Lilah. "We have reservations."

"Ready."

I hold out an arm and after an instant of confusion, puts in her hand in the crook of my elbow.

Blackie hops down and follows us to the door.

"You can't go with us, Blackie," she says, releasing my

arm to pick up the cat and hand him over to Bradley. "We'll be back."

"Your cat?" I ask.

"Not mine. Someone named Claire."

"Right. *That* cat."

Outside, I open the passenger door for her. She looks up, then back to me. "This might be difficult."

"Let me help you," I say.

"Okay." She puts a hand on the inside door arm, but I simply scoop her up in my arms, bridal style, and lift her up.

"Oh," she says as I place her gently on the seat.

"All good?"

"Yes." The word comes out a little breathlessly. With a smile, I close her door.

Obviously she's never had a man lift her into a truck before.

It seems, I muse, as I walk around the truck to the driver's side. I have quite a few advantages in my favor already.

With a girl like Lilah, I'm going to need every advantage I can get.

In the driver's seat, I look over at her. She's already buckled in. I buckle my own seatbelt.

"Ready?"

She nods. "You said we have reservations?"

"Yes. At the Whiskey Springs Lodge. They have the nicest restaurant in town."

"It must be to need reservations."

"Reservations aren't really necessary, but I wanted to make sure they weren't having any kind of event tonight."

"And if they did?" she asks.

"I'd figure something else out."

"It's good to be resourceful." She toys with the rose in her hands and looks straight ahead as I turn the truck around and head down the hill.

"We have cameras all along this road now," I say. "If anyone comes up to the house, you'll know."

"Audrey is worried about that."

"You're not?"

She shrugs. "I don't know what to think yet."

I drive around the big curve just before what I call the narrows. Everyone calls it something different.

"I do know that I don't like this road." Holding onto her seat, she looks down.

"No one does."

"They should fix it."

"I think Bradley's looking into it."

"Audrey told me you're a lumberjack."

"Did she now? It's just one of the things I do for my family's business."

"You have cabins and provide firewood."

"That's right. But I'm thinking of branching out and doing something different."

"Like what?"

"I'm thinking about building a greenhouse and opening a flower shop."

Good God. As soon as the words are out of my mouth, I wonder what the hell made me tell her that.

I'd suggested the idea to John at the General Store and it had somehow stuck in my head.

A flower shop. I don't anything about flowers.

The most I know about flowers is that you bring a girl a rose on a first date and if you like her, you turn it into a regular habit.

"Wow. That sounds... daunting," she says. "I don't know anything about flowers."

"Neither do I."

SIXTEEN

Lilah

EVEN OVER THE new car scent of the truck, I can tell that Wyatt smells like old leather and spruce trees. Outdoors. He smells like outdoors, but freshly showered beneath it.

Obviously knowing his way, he drives along the back-roads with nothing to light his way except for the truck's headlights and the soft glow of the full moon.

At the highway, he turns left, then turns left again before long.

According to the sign, we're approaching the Whiskey Springs Lodge.

"Wait," I say, shifting to look at him. "You don't know

anything about flowers, but you're thinking about opening a flower shop."

"Yes. There isn't one in town. I had to get that rose out of someone's backyard."

"Their backyard?" I ask skeptically, running a hand along the thorns.

"I had their permission. John, the guy who owns the General Store, didn't have any flowers, but he had some in his backyard."

"That's one of the strangest things I've ever heard. But it's nice." I run my hands along the stem, avoiding the thorns.

"That's why it doesn't have a ribbon or anything."

"It doesn't need it." I look at him, studying him beneath my lashes. "You sound like me."

"How so?"

"I knew nothing about mixed drinks, but I took a job as a bartender at an upscale bar."

"How did you manage?"

"I studied. I learned everything there is to know about liquor and wine and beer."

"Impressive."

"Yeah. Turns out it was all for nothing."

"Maybe not. You could open a bar."

"No thank you. Not a chance."

"And you don't know anything about flowers?"

"I like them," I say.

"But you could learn them."

"A person can learn about anything they want to."

"I like your optimism."

We turn a curve and the lodge comes into view.

It's a two story lodge with what looks like an attic serving as a third story.

"It's not what I expected," I say. "It's grand."

"They actually talked about calling it the Grand Lodge, but it didn't stick."

"It's very impressive. It looks like it's made out of real logs."

"It was. It's over a hundred and fifty years old."

"Looks like it's been kept up well. And there are a lot of cars here. It's a good thing you made a reservation."

"It's rather unusual. People usually come in on the train to stay here." He finds a spot and parks the truck.

"Maybe they're just having dinner."

"Maybe. Wait there. I'll come around."

I wait while he comes around to open my door, wondering if maybe I can just slide out.

My dress is too slim for me to step up with any dignity at all. Not that I minded being picked up and placed on the seat. Not that I minded that even a little.

He opens the door and smiles at me.

"Can I help you out of the truck, milady?"

My cheeks flush at the unexpected endearment. No one has every called me that before. "I think it might be the only dignified way for me to get out."

"Then I have a job to do," he says.

He scoops me up like I weigh no more than a child and set me down on my feet.

My heart racing, my hands are still resting on his shoulders, his hands are on my waist, and our gazes are locked onto each other.

"Thank you," I say, then clear my throat when the words come out a little rougher than I intended.

"My pleasure."

We both step back at the same time and he holds out his arm again. I put my hand in the crook of his elbow.

I could get used to this.

He's not even from the south and he acts like a perfect southern gentleman.

"Welcome, Mr. Winslow." The valet says as he opens the door for us.

So Wyatt Winslow comes to the lodge often enough to be recognized by name. Interesting.

Everything about Wyatt Winslow is interesting.

One look at him and my vow to myself to not date just shatters like a piece of glass into a million tiny unrecognizable shards.

CHAPTER
SEVENTEEN

Wyatt

It doesn't take long before I decide bringing Lilah to the lodge maybe wasn't the best idea in the world.

The lodge restaurant is nice. White tablecloths on the tables. Candles flickering on each one. Ambient lighting.

There's no doubt that it's a nice place to bring a date.

The downside is that everyone knows me here.

Still. I didn't want to drive down to Boulder. Spending over two hours driving isn't my idea of a way to spend a first date. This way I have more time to focus on her and not all my attention on driving.

I'm greeted by name by everyone starting with the valet. Then there's Zoe at the front desk as we pass by.

We pass Arabella as we walk across the grand lobby with the large four sided fireplace in the center with people taking advantage of the comfortable seating around it.

Lilah doesn't say anything about me being recognized by everyone and none of them linger long enough for me to introduce her. There will be plenty of time for me to introduce her to plenty of people as time goes by.

Right now I just want to get to a quiet table in the restaurant so I can be alone with Lilah.The hostess, a young lady I don't recognize, leads us, as I had requested, toward a table in the back right next to a fireplace with cozy gas flames.

I hold Lilah's chair while she sits down, then sit next to her.

A server, a young lady with her long hair pulled back in a ponytail high on her head, brings two crystal glasses and fills them with water from a matching pitcher. "What can I get you to drink?" she asks.

"What would you like, Lilah?" I ask.

"Water's good for me. Thanks."

"Water for me, too. Thanks." After the server walks away, I rest my elbows on the table. "I'm your designated driver if you'd like to take advantage of that."

"It's okay. It's bad form to drink on a first date."

"Really? When did they make that rule?"

She bites her lip and smiles. "I just made it up." She leans forward and lowers her voice. "I'm a lightweight."

"That's an interesting twist."

"A lightweight bartender. Not so rare as you would think."

"I actually never gave it any thought."

"So." She takes a sip of her water. "Tell me more about your flower shop."

"It's not really a thing. It's just something I thought of tonight when I went on a search for a flower for you."

"So I was your inspiration," she says with a little smile.

More than you will ever know. "I suggested it to John, the owner of the General Store. He's going to talk about it with his wife. But they should be thinking about retiring. Not starting their own business."

"A person's never too old to do what they want to do."

"Hm. But it was my idea. It wasn't something he would've thought about on his own."

She leans her arms on the table. "Then maybe you should do it."

I lean back in my chair, rubbing my chin. I know exactly where I'm headed with this conversation, but I don't want her to know that. Not yet.

"I would need someone who knows flowers."

She smiles. "You could learn."

"No." I say with mock seriousness. "I'm not that smart. I'd need help."

"I think you're smarter than you give yourself credit for."

I shrug. "Maybe. So far it's not working for me."

She picks up a menu. "I have a feeling you'll figure it out."

She knows good and well that I'm trying to get her to say she'll help me, but she's not falling for it.

Smart girl.

EIGHTEEN

Lilah

AFTER DINNER, Wyatt is quiet on the drive back to Audrey's house. I point that out to him.

"You got quiet."

I wouldn't classify Wyatt as a quiet person by nature. We talked throughout dinner without any lulls in the conversation.

Our conversation shifted away from the flower shop he may or may not be serious about opening. I've never looked into it, but it sounds like an incredibly big endeavor.

I just finished one big endeavor (the bartending fiasco) and I'm not ready to start another one.

I want to paint. I'm an artist and I want to paint.

We talked about everything and nothing.

My trip up to Whiskey Springs. How the weather is so very different between here and Houston. His family's cabins and how they're always renovating one cabin or another.

He keeps his eyes on the road as we head up the mountainside—a road I'd rather not travel at night, but so far I was doing it anyway.

"I got an alert on one of the cameras we just installed," he says. "But when I checked the history, there was nothing there."

"The ones on the road?"

"No. The one behind the house. Down by the river."

"There was nothing there?"

"Just a deer. And a couple of birds. I may have to change the settings."

"Maybe. Isn't it better to get a false positive?"

"You're right," he says, slowing down as we reach the cliff.

"There's really got to be a better road than this."

"There used to be an old road that circled around. Came around and avoided the narrows."

"Why on earth would they change it?"

"I think this is a shortcut."

"Sometimes it's best not to take shortcuts," I say,

keeping my eyes on the road as though that would help us avoid sliding off.

"Agreed."

"I'll ask Audrey to look into it. Maybe she can get the old road reopened."

"It would take a lot of money and influence to make that happen. I think someone bought that property."

"They bought the land where the old road is?"

"I think so."

"Well. She can just buy it back."

"Maybe. People tend to hold onto their land up here."

"You buy cabins all the time. How is that different?"

He parks the truck in front of the house. All the lights are out, even though it isn't all that late.

"I don't know. She can check it out. I've just noticed that people are more willing to sell land that has a house on it than straight up land. A house increases the taxes quite a bit."

"I see. I think everyone's asleep."

"They're like an old married couple," Wyatt says with amusement.

"They do seem to get along well, don't they?"

"I think Bradley is worried about rushing Audrey. It hasn't been all that long since she became a widow."

"He's got a good point. It hasn't been long. And I don't want to see her get hurt."

"Bradley won't hurt her. He likes her." He turns off the motor, leaving us in darkness.

"I hope so. She likes him, too."

"I'll come around. Help you out."

"Now I know what not to wear," I say as he opens my door.

"I like your dress. If you don't like me picking you up, I can help you slide out."

"It's okay." I hold out my arms. "We have it figured out now."

"Yes. We do. Don't we?"

He picks me up and lifts me right out of the truck. But this time, as he lowers me to the ground, he does it slowly, keeping me close.

For just a moment, my arms are around his shoulders and his arms around my waist.

He's taller than I thought he was. A full head taller.

The front porch light hums and pops on, bathing us in unexpected light.

"When did they do that?" he asks, pulling back.

"I don't know. I just got here."

"I know. Let me walk you inside. Make sure everything is okay."

"Those notes really have everyone spooked," I say as we walk toward the front porch, illuminated in bright lights. "Do you really think these lights will keep whoever it is away?"

"I hope so. I'm not sure what more we can do than these lights and the cameras."

Reaching the door, I unlock it with the key Audrey gave me.

Wyatt, it seems, is quite invested in this thing, too. But, of course he is. His brother is involved.

We step inside the quiet house. The fire is banked. The lights are out.

Biscuit, lying in front of the fireplace, stirs. Blackie is lying on the sectional, surprisingly not far from the dog.

"They've already gone up to bed," I whisper.

"I'm just going to go out back. Check things out real quick."

"Okay. I'll get us some water."

Wyatt, quiet as a mouse, steps outside while I get us a couple of bottles of water from the refrigerator.

His definition of real quick and my definition are different. He seems to be taking his time.

I sit on the sectional next to Blackie and scratch the cat's head. Blackie stretched as turns over.

The seconds tick by.

Wyatt should be back by now.

I said I wasn't sure if I was spooked about the notes, but now all the scary movies I've watched come back to haunt me. The ones where the guy goes outside to check on things only to be killed by the bad buy while the unsuspecting girl waits inside.

I'll give him another minute before I go check on him.

That minute passes quickly.

I pick up the poker next to the fireplace, take a

moment to get used to its weight in my hand, then start toward the back door.

I'm honestly not sure if I should open it or lock it.

Unfortunately, I like Wyatt, so I can't just lock him out.

This is how the bad guys get us.

Wyatt

I STEP out the back door and just stand there in the cool night air. The full moon is behind the clouds, so I'll have to wait until the clouds shift before I can see anything.

Even though I didn't see anything particularly unusual on the security cameras, the fact that an alert went off at all has me feeling unsettled.

This is the first time we've gotten an alert and yet I know it's not the first time there's been wildlife out here.

I wait patiently for the wind to shift. No surprising security lights out here just yet. I'll find out what Bradley needs help with and help him tomorrow.

We need to get all the systems in place to keep whoever is making these threats away from here.

Finally, after what seems like forever, the clouds shift, letting the light from the full moon shine through.

I walk to the edge of the back deck, carefully scan for anything that looks out of place, then turn around and study the house.

And then I see it.

A letter lying next to the back door.

"How are you doing this?" I ask under my breath.

I stride back to the door, pick up the letter, and slowly open the backdoor so as to not make any noise.

And there, right behind the door, is Lilah, standing there with a fireplace poker in her hands.

"What are you doing?" I ask.

"You didn't come back," she says, lowering the poker.

"I had to wait for the clouds to clear."

"You found something."

"Yes." I flip the backdoor lock and follow her back to the fireplace where she replaces the poker.

"What does it say?"

I sit down on the sectional and tug out the flap. She sits next to me.

I read aloud.

"You think there's safety in numbers. All you're doing is just putting more people at risk. This house doesn't belong to you. It doesn't belong to any of you. Don't ever forget that."

"Wow," she says. "I don't know what to say."

"It's bold."

"We need to give it the police."

"The police consists of a sheriff and he's an idiot."

"What other options are there?"

"I think the best option is catch whoever is doing it in the act."

"Wyatt. There are cameras at the back of the house. Cameras along the road. How could someone get past all the cameras?"

"I haven't figured that out yet. We will, though. We'll figure it out. There are four of us now and we'll figure it out."

I stare into the banked fireplace and wonder. I'm missing something. I have to be missing something. But I just don't know what it is.

"I'll leave this note on the kitchen island for them to see in the morning." I look over at Lilah. So beautiful. And there's a madman running around making threats. Distracting me from the simple act of appreciating her.

"Come on," I say. "I'm walking you up to your room."

"You don't have to do that."

"I'd feel better if you let me check your room. Then lock it behind you before I leave."

"I'm not afraid," she says, but the little shiver that runs through her says otherwise.

I take her hand and together we walk upstairs. My

brother's door is wide open. I can't but notice he's there sleeping in his bed.

Audrey's door is cracked, but not open all the way.

My brother is keeping his promise to stay here and protect her.

"This is my room," Lilah says. "Here at the end of the hallway. I have the best view."

We step inside and I see that she does, indeed, have a good view. Not that I can speak to the other views. I've never been up here before.

I check the bathroom. The closet. Even under the bed. While Lilah watches me with an expression I can't read.

"All clear," I say.

"Thank you."

I take her hands in mine. "You don't have to thank me."

"But I want to."

"Lilah," I say. "Call me anytime day or night. Anytime anything doesn't feel right."

"Okay." She nods. "But... I don't have your phone number."

I pull a business card out of my wallet. Hand it to her. "Promise me."

"I promise. But there are two other people here."

"They might not always be here."

"You're right." She shoves her hair back off her face with her hand. "Thank you for a lovely evening."

I cup her delicate chin in my hand.

She looks at me with green eyes that remind me of a mountain meadow. I just tumble right over into them.

Slowly lowering my face to hers, I pause as she tips her face up, her eyes fluttering closed, her lips parting.

It's enough.

I press my lips lightly against hers.

She leans into me, deepening the kiss.

Pulling back, she looks at me, her eyes wide, biting her lip. "Sorry," she says. "I'm sorry. I shouldn't have done that."

"Don't be," I say, pulling her into my arms and kissing her again.

I feel her yield to me and I deepen the kiss, kissing her bottom lip. Her top lip.

I don't want to let her go. But now isn't the time to get lost in her kisses. To get lost in her.

I kiss her on the forehead. "I'll see you tomorrow," I say.

"Okay." Her expression is soft. Vulnerable.

Beautiful.

I slide my hands down her arms and squeeze her hands.

"Lock your bedroom door behind me. I'll let myself out."

I walk away while I still can.

The only thing keeping me from turning right back around is knowing I'll see her tomorrow.

TWENTY

Lilah

I STAND in the middle of my bedroom, watching Wyatt turn and walk away.

"Lock the door," he says over his shoulder before he closes it.

In a daze, I follow him to the door and lock it. It doesn't seem right, really, locking myself in when my sister is out there with her door open.

But she's got Bradley to watch after her.

Maybe Wyatt is right about me needing to stay in here and stay safe. Bradley can't be responsible for me when he's watching over my sister. Either way, I'm too exhausted to argue.

Not only exhausted, but I feel like I'm in a dream world.

I'd been wanting to kiss him since I'd first looked into his eyes, but now that I had, it was so much more than I expected.

My lips still tingle from the feel of his against mine.

Going into the bathroom, I look at myself in the mirror. My lips are pleasantly swollen from his kisses.

It's not just his kisses that has my lips curving into a little smile. It's the promise of more of them.

Unspoken promises of more to come. That's what he had given me.

I can live with unspoken promises.

As I change into my pajamas and wash my face, I replay the night.

Being around Wyatt has my blood racing through my veins and yet at the same time, I feel safe with him.

Safe.

Not exactly something I should be feeling right now.

I'd actually gone all evening without thinking about the possible lawsuit hanging over my head. Two years. I have two years to worry about that woman pressing charges against me.

Two years before I can completely let go of what happened with Trey and the damage that had done to me.

When I'm with Wyatt, all that stuff that happened to

me... Trey... Bernice... Natalie... seems like something that happened to someone else.

For a few short hours, I was able to put it aside and think about something else. To be someone else. To be the person I really am.

To be happy.

Wyatt makes me happy.

I didn't come out here to my sister's house to find someone who made me happy. I'd come out here to put my old life behind me.

And now that I'm here, I find out my sister needs me. Someone is leaving sinister and threatening notes for my sister.

There's even one she doesn't know about downstairs on the kitchen island.

Even after the guys had installed cameras, someone managed to get past them. But how?

It's almost like whoever left the notes is a ghost.

Why would someone want us gone from here? It has to have something to do with the inheritance. Someone else feels entitled to the inheritance.

The only person who comes to mind is Thomas's baby momma, but she's in Houston taking care of a child. She couldn't get up here to Whiskey Springs, much less leave notes on the doorstep. It's not her. I'm certain of it. That doesn't even add up. She got Thomas's insurance money and all the other money he had put away for the child.

Definitely not her.

Audrey mentioned something about the old man Albright having a brother.

Now that made sense.

I climb into bed and turn on the lamp.

I pick up Wyatt's business card and study it. Just his name, a phone number, and *Timber Ridge Cabins and Timber Co.*

No title.

I put his number in my phone and set it on the charger.

About two minutes later, I pick up my phone and send him a text.

Me: Just letting you know I have your number in my phone. This is Lilah. Good night.

My finger hovers over the send button. Playing with fire. That's what I'm doing.

There's plenty of fire where Wyatt is concerned.

I'm doing exactly what I'd said I wasn't going to do.

I've barely even arrived and already I'm getting close to another man.

Wyatt deserves better than someone who could be hauled off to jail at any minute.

I hit send.

I can't help myself.

He sends a message right back.

Wyatt: And now I have your number. Sweet dreams, Milady.

With a smile on my lips, I put my phone back on the charger.

Nope. I can't help myself.

Not even a little.

TWENTY-ONE

Wyatt

I GET BACK to Audrey's house just before nine the next morning.

Bradley leads me back to the breakfast table where he and Audrey are huddled over their morning coffee and from what I'm sensing, they've been in deep conversation.

"Thanks for the heads up," Bradley says.

"Sure thing." I sent Bradley a message about the note I'd found so he'd have it when he woke up this morning.

But, being the light sleeper that he is, and the responsible older brother who keeps his phone on all the time, he'd gotten the message right away.

I'd been on the phone with him when he walked downstairs just before Midnight to read the note.

He had decided not to wake Audrey up to tell her. A very good idea and if I hadn't been afraid she would wake up first and find it, I wouldn't have messaged him as soon as I got home.

In hindsight, I could have taken the note with me or left it with Lilah, but it wasn't ours to decide.

Audrey looks well-rested despite the stress of finding a new note had been left for her.

"Good morning, Wyatt," she says. "Do you want coffee?"

"Sure. That would be great."

She slides out of her seat and gets to work making me coffee on her fancy coffee machine.

"I thought the cameras would have put a stop to all this," she says, handing me a mug of coffee and sitting back down.

"We all did," Bradley says.

"In a perfect world, it should have." I take the first sip of my second cup of coffee for the day. "Good coffee."

"Somehow they got past all our cameras."

"Did you go back and look?" I ask my brother. "See if you could find anything? Any gaps in time?"

"I did and I didn't see any time gaps. We both looked. We've been up since five o'clock."

"If they were trying to disrupt your life, they should be happy."

"Do you think whoever is leaving these notes is dangerous?" Audrey asks, running her fingers along her mug.

"We won't allow them to hurt you. Or Lilah," Bradley says.

"There has to be a way to at least find out who's doing it," I say.

"The sheriff ran the prints," Audrey says. "He's certain it's Claire. Her prints. But it can't be Claire. She's in jail. We should take this note in. Let him run it for prints."

"He's an ass hat," I say. "Even if Claire's prints are on it, doesn't mean she did it. She could have easily been set up."

"Or he could be lying about it," Bradley says.

"Exactly," I say.

At the sound of a door opening upstairs, I look toward the top of the stairs. Biscuit gets up from where he was sleeping in front of the fireplace. Shakes himself and races to the stairs.

Lilah stops.

"Biscuit," Bradley says. "Come here." Biscuit races over to Bradley. "Leave Lilah alone."

"Lilah's afraid of dogs," Audrey says.

"I'm not afraid," Lilah says, coming down the stairs.

Her gaze finds mine and holds. She looks a bit surprised to see me.

"Good morning," she says. Then shifts her gaze to her sister. "I'm just wary of dogs who look like small horses."

"She makes a good point," I say in her defense.

"Biased," Bradley says.

Lilah looks at me questioningly as she goes straight to the coffee machine.

"I told you I'd see you today."

"I know, but it's still so early."

I don't answer. Anything I can think to say involves pointing out that she's not only up, but showered, dressed, and her hair is freshly blow dried. She's even wearing light makeup.

"We're trying to figure out how to catch whoever is leaving these notes," I say in explanation for why I'm here.

"Cameras didn't stop him," she says.

"I'm not sure there's anything we can do," Audrey says, with a sigh.

"Don't give up," Bradley tells her. "We'll figure something out.

"Are the notes always left at night?" Lilah asks, bringing her cup of coffee over and sitting in the chair next to mine.

"Except for the one that was left in Audrey's book," Bradley says.

"And there's always some kind of noise, alerting you," she says.

"Except last night. Last night we didn't hear it."

"And I'd already taken Biscuit out for his walk," Bradley says.

"It's almost like he was watching and waiting."

"We should watch and wait for him," Lilah says.

"How?" we all ask at the same time, looking at her.

She sets her mug down.

"Like Wyatt said, there are four of us now. We set up a stakeout. Two of us watching the back and two watching the front. He might can get past cameras, but we should be able to see some sign of whoever's doing it."

"That's what we'll do," Bradley says. "We'll wait up for the son-of-a-bitch tonight."

"But not to confront. Just to take pictures," Audrey says.

I exchange a glance with Bradley and neither one of us says anything.

We can't guarantee we won't confront the ass hat who's doing this.

"I'm sure they'll be safe," Lilah tells Audrey. "whatever they do."

"I'm sure," Audrey murmurs behind her coffee mug.

Blackie jumps off the sectional and walks over to sit at Lilah's feet.

"Hey, little guy." She runs a hand over the cat's back, then looks at Audrey. "Has he eaten today?"

"Not yet."

Lilah scoops up the cat and puts him on the kitchen

island. Fills a bowl with cat food. The cat gobbles it up like he hasn't eaten in days.

"You'll have to feed him up here," she says. "Someone will eat his food." She looks pointedly at Biscuit.

"He doesn't know any better," Bradley says in his dog's defense.

"So," I say. "Are we going to get those security lights installed in the back?"

"We'll do that this morning," Bradley says. "Then you'll be happy to know that the window shades came in."

"Great," I say with a groan. Window shades. Installing window shades are not my idea of fun. But they have to be done.

Anything to stop these insane threats.

TWENTY-TWO

Lilah

THE MEN DECIDE to divide and conquer.

Bradley gets started on installing the living room window shades with Audrey right there with him. The two of them work in a rhythm they apparently must have established fairly quickly. They act like they've known each other forever, even though in reality it's only been less than a month. I knew Audrey had done some things around her house in Katy, but I'd never actually seen her doing them.

It throws me off just a little. Seeing this side of my sister I haven't seen before.

Wyatt is the self-appointed electrical guy. He hauls three brand new motion sensor lights, still in the box, a ladder, and a drill out to the back of the house.

I put away the coffee mugs. Wipe off the table and counter with a damp cloth.

I don't need to get in Audrey and Bradley's way. They don't need my help. And I honestly don't care to be a third wheel.

After watching Wyatt out the window for a few minutes, I decide he doesn't need any help either.

With everyone working, I can't just gather up my paint supplies and head out, as much as I might want to.

Besides, I'd rather find an excuse to spend time with Wyatt.

Unfortunately, I know nothing about installing lights so I can't exactly genuinely offer to help him with installing the lights.

With nothing left to do but listen to Audrey and Bradley discussing their work as they go, I step out onto the back porch where Wyatt is perched on a ladder.

"Hey," Wyatt smiles. "I'm glad you're here."

"Yeah?" My heart skitters a bit.

"Would you hand me that cup of screws?"

"Sure." Not exactly what I was hoping for. But I can hand things up.

I grab the only cup of screws in sight and hand them up to him.

"Thanks," he says. "Keep me company?"

"Okay." I sit down on the nearest chair. "It's a beautiful day."

It's actually cool enough that I'm glad I have my sweatshirt on, but the sun is bright and warms the air.

"A lovely day for painting," he says. "You should go paint."

"That would be bad form," I say.

"How do you figure?" Wyatt asks, deftly drilling into the wall.

"Everyone is working. I should be helping."

"You know anything about electrical?" I shake my head. "How about hanging window shades?"

"I don't know anything about that either. Should I be learning?"

"As long as you can keep me company and hand me things, you're good."

"I can do that." I bite my lip. This is a better arrangement than I expected.

"That was a good idea you had," he says, twisting two wires together.

"Which one?"

"The one about setting up a stakeout."

"Might be a little bit dangerous."

"I don't think so. We'll take the back of the house while Audrey and Bradley take the front."

"How do you think we're going to actually do it?"

He glances at me. Shrugs. "We'll set up at the windows. Anything moves, we'll see it."

I nod. "We can watch the cameras, too."

"We could. But the cameras are recording and so far they haven't given us anything. I think we try eyes on. If we see anything, we go back and look at the recordings."

"It might work."

"We're going to catch him," Wyatt says with all the confidence of a man who never fails at anything. "There's no way a person can keep dropping notes off and not get caught. We've got too many cameras. And with these motion sensor lights, we should most definitely catch him red-handed."

"Or frighten him away," I say.

"I'm thinking that would be okay, too."

I gaze toward the tree line, wondering how someone could be so bold as to walk right up to someone's door to drop off threatening notes.

"It has to be someone who knows the area and isn't afraid to walk around in the woods after dark," I say.

"I don't know where he parks. But finding a parked car is another way to go about it."

"He could park anywhere. How far is the walk between here and town?"

"It would be a hike," Bradley says. "But it could be done. There are a few cabins between here and there."

I pull my feet up under me and rest my chin on my

palm. "Any cabins that you're renting to someone? Within walking distance?"

Bradley stops. Looks at me. "Not sure. I'll have to check into that."

"Lots of possibilities."

"You've got a good head on your shoulders." He goes back to twisting wires together.

"It's all that time I spent exercising my brain learning to be a bartender."

"Just think how smart you could be if you'd learn about flowers."

I narrow my eyes at him. "Good try. But that sounds like a major endeavor."

"It would be. But I'd make it worth your while."

"And how exactly would you do that?"

"Haven't figured that out yet." He skins a wire and twists it to attach it to another one.

"Well," I say. "Let me know when you do."

"Thought you weren't interested."

"I was planning on coming out here to paint," I say, scanning the area, halfway expecting to see something or another move. Some kind of movement. Anything.

Wyatt leans his arms on the top of the ladder. "I'm getting the idea you're a lot like me."

"How so?"

"I'm getting the feeling you can't resist a challenge."

I smile up at him. "You are right about that."

But what I can't tell him is that I'm damaged goods.

One word from Bernice and I'll be summoned back to Houston to do my time in jail for assault.

Assault with wine. Whoever would have thought?

I can't tell him. It's too embarrassing. I can't even tell Audrey.

The only person who knows is Brianna.

And she's sworn to secrecy.

I guess I don't have anyone to blame but myself. I'd done it. I'd tossed the wine into Bernice's face. So I have to live with it.

It's what I get for being so sensitive about what happened with Trey. The whole thing left me feeling icky.

Rubbing my hands over my arms, I push the memories away. I'd like to shove them down into a deep dark hole, but things keep happening to bring them back to the surface.

I have a plan. My plan is to hide out here for two years and hope it goes away.

In the meantime, I can practice my art.

I sigh. Not thinking about whether or not painting is allowed in jail. Drawing. I can work on my drawing. All I have to do is commit everything I see to memory.

Making my living as an artist is my dream fantasy. In reality I know how unrealistic it is. At least for now. While I'm here, I have to do my part to pull my weight.

I'll figure something out.

The only thing I know for certain it won't be is bartending. That left a really bad taste in my mouth.

I glance up to find Wyatt watching me.

He winks at me and a whole bevy of butterflies lets loose in my stomach.

Maybe there's something about the fresh mountain air that affects us Sinclair girls.

Makes us lose our senses.

TWENTY-THREE

Wyatt

THE DARKNESS of night brings thunderstorms and rain coming down in sheets, bringing a misty fog with it.

"I think we should postpone our stakeout," I say over ham sandwiches in the breakfast room. "No one is going to come out in this storm to drop off threatening notes on the doorstep."

"No," Bradley says. "I don't want to risk it."

Lilah and Audrey look at each other, exchanging some sisterly language only known to them.

"A person would have to be insane to be out in this weather."

"Let's think about that for minute," Bradley says. "Only an insane person would drop notes off to start with."

"Okay," I say, glancing at Lilah. "Good point."

I can think of worse ways to spend an evening than hanging out with Lilah, even if it does involve sitting upstairs in an unoccupied bedroom looking out over the backyard.

Audrey and Bradley will be in the attic watching the front porch area.

"It's dark," Audrey says. "He always leaves the notes after dark."

Despite the sheriff's insistence that Claire was the one who had been leaving the notes, the four of us agreed that it had to be a man. Only a man would come out in the woods at night to drop notes off at the door.

Two notes dropped off at the front door. One in a small jewelry-sized box. The other in an envelope. One note dropped off at the back door, also in an envelope.

Then there was the note in Audrey's book and the flowers with no note. Since the note in the book and the flowers left on the kitchen island required further explanation, we didn't include them in tonight's search parameters.

Lilah starts picking up empty plates.

"We'll clean up later," Audrey says.

"It won't take but a minute." Lilah already has the plates gathered up and is carrying them to the sink.

"I'll help you," I say. A rumble of thunder reminds us that we're in the middle of a thunderstorm. And I maintain my stance that a person would be crazy to be out here during this weather.

She was right. It only takes a minutes for us to have everything in the dishwasher.

Lilah even takes a cloth and wipes the table.

"Habit," she says.

"It's a habit you should consider picking up," Bradley says to me.

I shoot him a withering glance.

"Okay," Audrey says. "Bradley and I are going to be upstairs. Phones on silent. If you see something and can't call, text." She looks at Lilah. "Record everything that moves."

Lilah gives her a thumbs up. No one reminds her that we already have camera on every angle.

"I guess we're heading up to our location, too," I say.

Leaving Biscuit sleeping front of the fireplace and Blackie curled up on his end of the sectional, the four of us head upstairs, for all appearances, heading up to our respective bedrooms.

With the new shades pulled down over the windows, hiding the stunning views of the snow-capped mountains, a casual observer might even draw the conclusion that Lilah and I are hanging out in front of the fireplace. We'd left the television on to flicker along with the flames from the fireplace.

Audrey's nightstand reading light is on, just like it always is this time of night.

"Biscuit will bark before any of us see anything," Bradley says as he and Audrey veer off toward the attic stairs.

"I think he's down for the night," Lilah says.

"Never underestimate the power of a dog's hearing," I tell her as we enter the unoccupied bedroom.

Like the other bedrooms in the house, it's fully furnished with a king-sized bed. An inviting white comforter and pillows. A nightstand with a lamp. An unadorned dresser.

And most importantly at the moment...

Two windows. Two chairs.

She and I take our seats, just off to the side of either window, turned slightly to face each other.

We'd set the chairs up earlier, deciding this gave us the best view.

"It's hard to see anything in the darkness," Lilah says. "with the storm.

A flash of lightning punctuates her words.

"I think someone might have mentioned that," I say, but I keep my eyes fixed on the tree line. Each flash of lightning cuts through the darkness, revealing the branches thrashing in the wind.

"You did. But Bradley isn't wrong. Anyone crazy enough to do this to begin with, is probably crazy enough to not let a little bad weather stop them."

"We'll see."

We're both holding our phones. Both staring out the windows.

"I hope the motion lights don't scare him away," Lilah says. "I really want us to bust his ass."

"I couldn't have said it better myself," I say with obvious appreciation.

"Sorry." She winces.

"No need to apologize. I agree with you one hundred percent."

Rain slams into the windows and thunder crashes along with streaks of lightning.

I keep my opinion to myself. There's crazy. And then there's crazy.

Coming out in this kind of weather would take a whole different level of crazy.

Lilah

I STARE through the window trying to see anything in the blinding rain until my eyes hurt.

What kind of person would come out in this rain to leave a threatening note?

The kind of person who would threaten someone to begin with.

I can't help but worry that the notes are just the first step for whoever is doing this.

Hopefully they're just idle threats.

The problem is there is more at stake than just the ownership of the house.

Wyatt, and not even Bradley know that the house is part of a package deal.

Whoever has possession of the house also receives a one million dollar annual stipend. The two go hand in hand.

A million dollars a year is a lot of money.

It's enough money that it's hard to say what lengths someone would go to in order to get Audrey, and now me by association, out of here.

A smart bad guy would go after me.

Putting me in danger would be one of the fastest ways to get Audrey to give up the house.

I really think Wyatt and Bradley should know that the stakes are higher than they know about.

"How far do you think someone would go?" I ask him. "to get Audrey out of the house?"

"I don't know. I guess it has something to do with how bad they want this place."

"Right. What if it's more than just the house?"

"Like what?"

I want to tell him about the money. I truly believe that the money is a big part of the whole thing. But it's not my place.

"Maybe it's about the Albright legacy," I tell him.

"I guess it could be," he agrees, but I can tell he doesn't think that has anything to do with it. "I don't understand the why of it. If someone has a right to it, why don't they contest it in court? We may never understand the why of it. I just want to find out who's doing it so we can put a stop to it."

"Right," I say, distractedly. Was that a movement there at the tree line? I lean closer toward the window before I remember we're trying to stay out of sight.

"See something?" he asks.

"I don't know. I don't think so. Probably just the wind."

Wyatt picks up a pair of binoculars and aims them toward the tree line. "It's too dark."

I tighten my sweatshirt around me and stifle a yawn.

The grandfather clock in the foyer begins to chime the eleven o'clock hour.

Wyatt lowers the binoculars. "If you want to go ahead and go to bed, I'll keep watch here."

"No. It's okay."

"There's a bed right there. You can take a nap."

A bed I'm trying not to think about. About being alone in a bedroom with Wyatt. "I often work late. I should be used to staying up late."

"You're still adjusting to the time difference. And don't discount the higher elevation."

"The elevation," I say, feeling a distinct aha moment going off in my head.

"A lot of people stay sleepy until they adjust to the elevation."

"That makes perfect sense," I say, fighting back another yawn. "I have been sleepy since I got here. I thought I was just tired from...everything." Being fired. Driving for days. Having the threat of a lawsuit hanging over my head.

"Probably a combination," he says, picking up his binoculars again.

"Have you ever lived anywhere else?" I ask. "Besides Whiskey Springs?"

"No." He sets the binoculars aside. "I commuted to college in Boulder, but I never lived there."

"You live with your parents?"

"God. No. I have my own cabin. Actually a cabin I'm renovating for the family."

"So you don't actually own a place of your own."

"Not exactly."

"Huh."

Two birds fly together toward us and we lose track of them as they duck under the covered porch.

"I didn't know birds cold fly in the rain," I say.

"I guess birds can fly in any conditions. But yeah. Normally they don't."

"What was your major?" I ask. "In college."

"Business. Of course. But it didn't really interest me. Our brother, Caleb, is the one who likes to be in charge of finances and such."

"It takes a different kind of personality to like numbers."

"I agree."

"What's Caleb like?"

The birds fly out from the covered porch and head back toward the tree line, staying low.

"He's charming. He's probably the reason we have so many cabins right now. Anytime someone is thinking about selling their property, he can seal the deal. He's especially charming to little old ladies." He takes a breath. "I mean that in the best possible way."

"I'm sure you do. Wyatt?"

"Yes?" He pulls his gaze away from the window and looks at me.

I swallow. "Speaking of meaning things in the best possible way."

He waits for me to keep going. I do so in a rush of words spilling out.

"With it raining like it is and dark, I'd feel a lot better if you slept here." I nod toward the bed. "Instead of driving along those deadly cliffs."

"I thought you'd never ask."

I smile and bite my lip.

We sit quietly a few more minutes, our gazes focused on the area below. Both of us straining to see the tree line obscured by the sheets of falling rain.

The wind shifts sending the soft rain slamming against the windows.

We hear Audrey and Bradley coming down from the attic.

They stop at our door.

"I think we can turn in. Pick up again tomorrow night," Bradley says. "We can check the cameras in the morning."

"Sounds good to me." Wyatt stands up.

"Is it okay if Wyatt sleeps in here tonight?" I ask Audrey. "The weather is too dangerous for him to driving."

"I hope he does. I hope he doesn't try to drive down the mountain in this." She looks at Wyatt with that older sister look that means she's telling him he's staying here.

"Much appreciated," he says.

"We'll get up early," Bradley tells his brother. "Get to work on those shades."

"They're tedious, aren't they?" he asks.

"Very tedious," Audrey says, looking at me. "I think I just got fired."

"I think not," Bradley says, pulling her close. "I just think your time could be better spent doing something else."

"He should run for sheriff," Wyatt says.

"I agree," Audrey says. "He would be good at it."

"I don't know what I did to get you two on that kick," Bradley says. "I'm not interested in running for sheriff."

I smile and keep my thoughts to myself. I learned a long... long time ago not to say I wouldn't do something. I learned that that thing I said I wasn't going to do was the very thing I ended up doing.

Of course, Bradley might not have that problem. Maybe it's just me.

I do one thing for certain. I'm going to sleep a whole lot better tonight knowing that Wyatt is in the bedroom next to mine.

CHAPTER
TWENTY-FIVE

WYATT

"I'll go with you to walk Biscuit," I tell Bradley as we head downstairs.

"He's not going to like getting out in this."

Lilah and Audrey are already headed down the stairs in front of us to feed Blackie in his designated spot on the kitchen island. As an older cat, he has a little route he uses to get up there. Jumping from a chair to a barstool, then up onto the counter where he eats right in the center of the island, away from Biscuit's access.

Bradley and I grab jackets from pegs next to the back door and he grabs a towel for Biscuit.

"Biscuit. Come on. Out." Biscuit runs over as soon as

Bradley opens the door, but seeing the rain outside, stops and looks up at him.

"I didn't do it," Bradley says. "Go on."

"Dog's too smart," I say, stepping outside behind my brother. Biscuit runs reluctantly out into the rain, but we stay underneath the covered part of the deck.

Biscuit's movements set off the motion sensor lights.

"Lights are working," he says.

"Of course."

"I think the rain is slacking off."

"Wishful thinking," I say. "I think it's settled in for the night."

Bradley puts his in hands in his jacket pockets. "Probably." He glances around like we all do now. "Didn't see anything?"

"Nah. Just a couple of birds."

"Yeah. We tracked an elk."

"The wildlife isn't used to this kind of weather," I say.

"A bit unusual. Global warming."

"Doesn't feel warm to me," I say, pulling my jacket tighter.

"How are things with your future wife?"

"Going good. Couldn't be happier."

"You're in what? Day two? Haven't changed your mind?"

"Not going to."

Tendrils of mist hover over the ground and white clouds with dark edges linger in the valley.

"Snowing up in the high country."

"Maybe."

Biscuit comes running back. Stops next to us and shakes before Bradley can get the towel over him, sending a spray of water over us.

"Payback," I say.

"The fastest he's ever done his business." Bradley tosses the towel over Biscuit and dries him off. "Hold still."

"At least we didn't get any threats tonight." I look around, even though I know there's nothing there. We've been watching.

"Just waiting for the other shoe to drop." Bradley opens the door and Biscuit shoots inside, heading right back to his spot on a rug in front of the fireplace.

"Anybody want a glass of wine?" Audrey asks.

"I'll take one," Bradley says.

"Just a sip," Lilah says. "to be sociable."

"What she said." I slide my jacket off, hang it up, and go stand next to Lilah.

"You got a little wet," she said.

"Biscuit gave Bradley payback for sending him outside in the rain. I just happened to be standing there."

The four of us take our glasses of wine to sit on the sectional in front of the fireplace.

Bradley kneels in front of it, gets the flames going again. Stacks firewood in, making a big fire.

"I think the stakeout was a good idea," Audrey says. "We should do it again tomorrow."

"I agree," Lilah says, holding her wine, but not drinking.

I'm more of a beer guy, but I can drink wine when I need to.

Bradley dusts his hands on his jeans and looks at me.

"You up for it?"

"I'm all yours."

Lilah looks at me with her brow furrowed. "You don't have any extra clothes, do you?"

"It's okay. I'm sure my brother has something I can steal."

"I'm sure I have something you can *borrow*," Bradley says, taking Audrey's hand.

I look over at Lilah sitting next to me. One day I'll be allowed to reach over and take her hand.

"I'll be okay," I say with a little smile.

And I'm not talking about having something wear. I'm talking about the rest of my life.

CHAPTER
TWENTY-SIX

LILAH

FLAMES in the fireplace crackle as they devour the strategically laid stack of wood. Little sparks drift up the chimney as one log burns through and causes all the others to shift places.

Bradley gets up and, using a black iron poker, shoves them back into place, sending out more sparks in the process.

Outside, the rain continues to fall, slamming against the windows as the wind shifts. The rain brings cold air with it. Not unusual for this level of elevation, even if it is summer.

The heat from the fireplace warms the air all the way

over to the sectional where I sit next to Wyatt. The old black cat curled up between us. I scratch his ears and he purrs. A really nice, soothing purr. I think he likes me because I'm the only here who doesn't smell like dog.

I take a sip of my wine. Dark cherries, blackberries, and the faintest whisper of vanilla beneath a hint of oak from its barrel. I hadn't seen the bottle, but I'm thinking it's a Cabernet Sauvignon.

I'm not a wine taster and I have absolutely no training in wine tasting. But I've studied it and I taught myself what to look for.

I've got all this knowledge about wine and drinks, but since I'm not much of a drinker, I'm not sure what I'm going to do with it.

Most of the wines I know about I haven't even tasted. This just happened to be one that I had. I actually think Audrey had this wine at her house once. Maybe last Thanksgiving. I was well into my study of wines at the time, so it stuck with me.

Our lives are so very different now than they were last fall, I can barely see the connections between them.

Just the tiniest of threads connecting who she and I used to be with who we are now.

Being close sisters, though, is one thing that won't change no matter not.

It's just she's a widow now. A rich widow living in a huge house in the mountains just on the outskirts of Whiskey Springs, Colorado. She has a new boyfriend.

Bradley Winslow. And Bradley comes with a giant horse dog.

From what I can figure, Bradley has moved in here. No one has told me officially, but it looks like he's moved in under the guise of protecting her from a stalker.

That's something else about her. She has an unidentified stalker who leaves threatening notes at the front and back doors.

And now the two of them, Audrey and Bradley are the stewards of a cat that belongs to the woman the sheriff believes is the one leaving the notes.

What a tangled web they weave.

Then there's me.

I was fired from my job as an upscale bartender/hostess at the Hobby Center after which I immediately quit my other bartending job.

So I'm jobless. Not only that, but I've been accused of assaulting a woman by throwing wine in her face. Of course I did it in my capacity as a hostess while on the job.

So... fired.

And the woman—all I know about her is her name —Bernice has two years to decide whether she wants to press charges against me for tossing the wine in her face.

It doesn't matter that she started it.

Isn't that how it goes? The person standing up to the bully is more often than not the one who gets in trouble.

So after getting fired from one job and quitting the

other, I pack everything up, turn in the keys to my apartment, and drive up here to Whiskey Springs.

And now I've met Audrey's boyfriend's brother. Wyatt.

I'd vowed to myself that I wasn't going to date again, at least not until I've gotten past the two years that I could be hauled back to a Houston jail for abovementioned assault with wine.

And yet I haven't even unpacked yet—not my fault— and I've already kissed Wyatt.

And, as it would be, I can't stop thinking about kissing him again.

Biscuit, the very large horse dog, stirs in his sleep. He's addicted to lying in front of the fireplace. I can't blame him. I like sitting in front of it, too.

The old solid black cat, aptly named Blackie, is sleeping next to me, snoring softly.

Audrey and Bradley have a few of the new window shades installed. Motorized, of course. Did I mention that Audrey is quietly wealthy?

She hasn't even told Bradley about the million-dollar —annual—stipend that comes with living in the house.

She will, though.

She assured me that she would tell him when the time is right. They might be old and gray when that time comes, but she'll tell him. Besides, he's eventually going to start to wonder where her money is coming from.

I hide a yawn behind the back of my hand.

"You should get some sleep, Sweetness," Wyatt says, leaning close to whisper.

"I think you might be right," I say, holding out my wine glass. His is empty. "Do you want this?"

"It's only a sip," he says.

"I know."

"You're not going to drink it?"

"Not right now."

"Do you want me to save it?" he asks skeptically.

I lean over and whisper back to him. "Just drink it."

With a look I can't decipher, he downs it in one swallow.

My life has so gone in a direction I hadn't thought possible.

One weak moment combined with a spontaneous decision along with one of those instant connections with a good-looking small-town man and here I go. Watching myself falling all over again.

TWENTY-SEVEN

Wyatt

A QUIET EVENING sitting at home. I confess that's unusual for me.

Not my home. My brother's girlfriend's home. Still. At technically at home.

If I'm at home, my home, by myself, I usually at least have the television on. Sitting, just sitting, in front of a cozy fire with the girl who has all my attention focused on her is a bit different.

It's late, nearly eleven o'clock, and I guess that's why our conversations have lagged into silence.

Outside, the storm continues to rage as it moves off into the distance, but it left a steady rain behind.

Tomorrow I'm supposed to help Bradley continue to hang the motorized window shades. It seems like a shame to cover up the spectacular views of the snow-capped mountains, but I see the reasoning behind it.

Right now, anyone could be standing outside looking in at us through the windows. In light of the recent threatening notes someone has been leaving on Audrey's doorstep, it's the logical thing to do. At night, anyway. I can see why she doesn't feel safe.

And now that I've claimed Lilah as my girl, in my head at any rate, I don't feel safe for her either.

So tomorrow Bradley and I will be doing the tedious job of hanging window shades. Not any easy job by any means, but with the two of us, and Audrey's help, we can knock it out.

Right now, though, it's time for me to get Lilah up to bed for some sleep.

Standing up, I hold out a hand.

"Can I escort you to your room, Milady?"

She blinks, telling me she's already halfway falling asleep and puts her hand in mine.

"Good night everyone," I say, linking my hand with Lilah's.

"Good night," Audrey and Bradley say together.

Biscuit stirs, but I don't think he's interested in going back outside right now. One trip out in the rain is probably enough for him for one night.

I lead Lilah toward the stairs. She yawns.

"I think you missed your bedtime."

"I think so, too." She wipes at her eyes. "Sorry. It's not you."

"I know."

She smiles up at me sideways. "A bit self-confident?"

I grin, squeezing her hand. "I know you're still adjusting the elevation."

We reach the top of the stairs and turn down the hallway toward our rooms. My room is first. Hers is at the end of the hallway.

We pass mine and keep walking.

"Thank you," she says.

"For what?" I take both her hands and shift her so that I'm looking into her meadow green eyes.

She shrugs. "I don't know. For being here."

"You don't have to thank me." I pull her close against me, cupping the back of her head with my hand.

The last thing she needs to do is to thank me.

She's got me under her spell. Bewitched. From the first moment I saw her.

Shifted a bit so I can look into her eyes again, I put a hand lightly beneath her chin.

"There's something I can't stop thinking about," I say, my throat tight.

She bites her bottom lip. "What's that?"

I lower my head and press my lips against hers in a kiss.

"This," I murmur against her lips. "I can't stop thinking about this."

Pressing my lips against hers again, I practically devour her with kisses.

This. This is what life is all about.

TWENTY-EIGHT

LILAH

THE NEXT MORNING dawns bright and sunny.

The air still has a slight dampness to it, but it won't last long. Unlike Houston, up here at this elevation, the air is dry. Even after a rain.

My first thought is Wyatt. Wyatt sleeping in the bedroom next door.

Somehow, even though it was supposed to just be Audrey living here alone, we've managed to fill up all four bedrooms of the house.

I stretch beneath the warm blankets, knowing that when I get up, the floors will be cold. I really, really like Audrey's idea of installing heated floors. The best use of that million dollar stipend that I've heard so far. Slippers. I need to order some slippers that I can wear around the house. The ones I have are old and ragged and I tend to forget and leave them in the bathroom.

It won't be long before Bradley will be moving into Audrey's bedroom. That will free up one of the bedrooms.

And Wyatt won't be here except on rare occasions. Like last night. I couldn't bear the thought of him driving along the cliffs with no visibility. It had been a bad storm. One of the worst in recent memory according to Bradley.

Our stakeout had been a bust just as Wyatt had predicted.

I could see Bradley's point, though, about whoever is leaving the notes being crazy. And if he's crazy enough to do that, he's most likely crazy enough to get out in the storm.

Maybe our stalker, the best word I can think of that fits what he's doing, has enough sense to stay in out of the rain after all.

I don't mind having another stakeout tonight as long as it involves spending time with Wyatt.

I'm slowly learning a lot about him. I wouldn't have pegged him for having a degree in business. Something, sure. But not business.

Business is far too boring for a guy who can install electrical lights and from what I understand, just about anything else that needs to be done around a house.

Bradley has a degree in engineering and it seems like

Wyatt would have done the same. It would fit him better and he even admits that a career in business didn't fit him.

If I were at home, by myself, I would have hit the coffee machine in my pajamas and hair that looks like birds made a nest in it overnight.

But that's not going to happen. Not with Wyatt in the house.

I turn on the water and give the shower time to heat up while I dig out a pair of blue jeans and a long-sleeve shirt from my suitcase.

Audrey has some kind of thing about closets. She wants to design all of them from a blank slate. I must be a simple girl with simple needs. I just need a place to hang a few clothes, some shelves, and I'm good.

I find it interesting that my first thoughts this morning were not about Trey or Bernice or the possibility of being dragged off to jail in Houston—currently my biggest fear.

Instead, my first thoughts are about Wyatt.

I can't decide how I feel about that. I feel good about it, but I feel guilty about feeling good about it.

I can't get too close to him. It wouldn't be fair to him.

Too late.

I step out of the shower sund towel off.

Having already kissed him is definitely too late to not get too close by anyone's definition.

It's bad, too, because I'm thinking I'm going to stay

here. I don't know how long. I can't just freeload on my sister even if she is loaded.

I don't have to decide right now.

Right now I have some other things to do.

After I dry my hair, I'm going in search of coffee.

Then I'll see what's going on with everyone else. If everyone else is working, I'll need to chip in. If not, I'll get some painting in.

Either way, I have very little doubt that I'll be bumping into Wyatt.

And that has my blood thrumming through my veins with anticipation and has me taking a few extra minutes to straighten my hair.

I examine my appearance in the bathroom mirror and declare myself ready to go downstairs. In my humble opinion, I look rather cute in my blue jeans, long sleeve shirt layered beneath a plain gray t-shirt, and my lace-up boots.

Coming from Houston, I most definitely don't have the right clothes for the mountains.

I've only been here a few days and I'm seeing that.

My heart racing, my palms a little bit damp, I wipe them on my jeans and open the door.

The first sound I hear is the sound of a drill. They're installing the window shades. Good. That's very important to Audrey. Understandably.

And I'm happy about it because Wyatt agreed to help.

I head downstairs, turning right to go straight to the

kitchen. I purposefully do not look to my left where everyone is working.

"Good morning, Sleepyhead," Audrey says.

"Hi." I pull a mug from the cabinet and get started making coffee in the fancy coffee machine.

"Did you sleep well?" she asks, coming over to join me.

"Actually. Yes. You know I love the sounds of a good rain storm."

"I know," she grins.

"How about you? Did you sleep well?"

"Yes," she says.

There's something she's not telling me. I glance over my shoulder just in time to catch Bradley whistling a happy little tune.

Things are most definitely moving along with those two. Just as I had predicted.

My coffee finished, I turn and lean against the counter.

Blackie uses his route to climb up on the chairs to the kitchen island, but instead of going for his food bowl, he comes right over to me. Holds one foot up and meows.

"Aw. Hi there." I go over and pet him, getting him going with that purr of his.

"He likes you," Audrey said.

"Where's Biscuit?" I ask, not seeing the horse dog in his place in front of the fireplace.

"Wyatt took him in to Boulder."

"Oh." Disappointment washes over me that Wyatt isn't here. "Why?"

"It's okay," she says, mistaking my disappointment that Wyatt isn't here to worry about something being wrong with the dog. "Some of our closet supplies came in and he went to get them. It was faster than having them shipped. Anyway, Biscuit likes to ride. And." She picks up a piece of toast. Takes a bite. "I think Wyatt wanted the company."

"That was good of him," I say. *I would have gone with him. I would have kept him company.*

"You weren't up yet," Audrey says with a smug expression. "And I asked him to pick up lunch on his way back."

"Lunch?"

"There's a seafood restaurant in Boulder that is supposed to have good seafood. That's one of the things I miss the most about Houston. The food."

I hide any comments I might have behind my coffee mug. If she had told me ahead of time, I could have gotten up to go with Wyatt.

Instead he took the dog.

Sometimes my sister is just clueless.

"Anyway," she says. "I thought you might want to get some painting done before lunch. After lunch, we're going to build closets. I thought you might want to help with that."

"Sure."

I'm rather glad she didn't put me in the position of choosing between painting and riding into Boulder with Wyatt.

As much as I love to paint, I have a very strong feeling that Wyatt would have won out this time.

TWENTY-NINE

Wyatt

EVEN THOUGH IT'S a beautiful day for it, I had not planned on driving into Boulder today.

If I had planned on driving into Boulder today, I would asked Lilah to join me.

Most definitely a missed opportunity, but not by my choosing.

Audrey asked me to pick up the things she ordered for the closets and she asked me to pick up lunch on the way back. She even wrote down the lunch order for me.

I took one look at my brother, wearing his tool belt,

getting ready to climb up a ladder and install window shades to know I was getting the best deal.

I didn't even mind Biscuit coming along even if I did have to stop halfway into the city to take him for a walk.

After that particular stop, the dog and I had a conversation that led to an additional, unplanned stop at the pet store.

My brother might not like it, but this was between me and the dog.

Driving back toward Whiskey Springs, sipping a milk shake that I'd gotten at the seafood restaurant, I admire the wildflowers, mostly blue and white scattered about the meadow.

My first thought is that Lilah would like to paint them.

All that gets me thinking even more about the flower shop idea I had so blithely tossed out there to John at the General Store.

A flower shop really is a missing staple in the little town of Whiskey Springs. Besides the General Store, we've got just about everything else a town could want. A coffee shop. An ice cream shop. Even a bookstore.

But if you want fresh flowers you have to either make a drive, get someone to make the drive to bring in a delivery, or go into someone's backyard.

We *need* a flower shop in town.

The fact that I don't know anything about flowers normally would have put a damper on the idea.

But Lilah said something that I can't let go.

A person can learn about anything they want to.

So simple and I'm not even sure I believe it. But I don't *disbelieve* it. And therein lies the problem.

John showed some interest, but he and his wife should be retiring. Not taking on a new venture like that.

As hard as I try, I can't think of anyone who would want to take it on. There's the lodge. They could handle it and it's probably most logical for them to do it, but damn it, it was my idea and I want to explore it before I just give it away.

Being the youngest child in a family that came with a ready-made business wasn't easy. People always just assumed that I would work in the family business. Not own it or anything like that. That's Bradley's job as the oldest. But work in it. To just be part of the family business.

Lilah changed the way I'm thinking about it.

Lilah made me start thinking that maybe there's no reason why I can't be the one to start a flower shop in town.

To even entertain the idea, I have a LOT of research to do.

If I can get Lilah interested, she and I could do the research together.

I can actually see myself relying on her maybe a little bit too much.

That's a good enough reason for me to let it go.

If I can't do it on my own, then I don't need to even be thinking about it.

Unless... unless I were to make Lilah an equal partner.

As I turn off the highway onto the road leading up to the Albright house, aka Audrey's house, Biscuit sits up and looks out the window.

"You know we're almost home, don't you?" I ask him.

He barks once in agreement.

"Home." What the hell is wrong with me? I'm not supposed to be thinking of Audrey's house as home.

I blame Lilah for that.

Lilah, the green-eyed goddess who's gotten under my skin.

CHAPTER
THIRTY

Lilah

Audrey encouraged me to take the morning for painting, but the ground is still damp from last night's storm. That's my story and I'm sticking with it.

It has nothing to do with wanting to be around when Wyatt gets back.

Besides, it's too cold outside for my paints.

I set up at the kitchen table with a sketch pad and pencils to sketch whatever catches my eye.

I start with the obvious. The rugged mountains in the distance. Capture their forever cap of snow draping down until it blends into the tree line. Aspen trees with their fluttering, musical leaves. Maple trees with their big, bold leaves. Spruce trees with their Christmas-tree like shapes.

With a sigh, I turn the page in my sketchbook and look around, closer in.

A blue bird sits perched on a pine tree limb at the edge of the deck. Knowing he won't sit there for very long, I slowly pick up my phone and snap a photo. Just as I expected, I'd no more than taken the photo when he flies off.

It's okay. I've got his photo. I zoom in on the photo and focus on sketching him.

Even over the sounds of Bradley and Audrey talking through their process of measuring and drilling as they hang the window shades, I hear Wyatt's truck coming down the road toward the house.

By the time he parks and I hear the car door slam, I have my sketching supplies tucked away.

While Audrey and Bradley go to meet him outside, to help him bring things in, I pull out my hair tie and let my hair sweep over my shoulders.

Even though my heart is pounding crazy in anticipation at seeing Wyatt again, I pull out four bottles of water and set them on the dining table along with napkins.

With that done, I wander toward the front door just in time to see Biscuit hop down from the passenger side of the truck.

"What have you done to my dog?" Bradley asks.

"Maybe you should talk to your dog about that," Wyatt says.

Biscuit is wearing a brand new harness and leash.

"What happened, Biscuit?" Audrey asks as the horse dog puts his front legs on Audrey's shoulders and licks her face. My sister, much to my surprise, just laughs and lets the dog lick her face.

Maybe she's not the same obsessive-compulsive Audrey I grew up with.

"He doesn't seem to mind wearing it," Bradley says.

"It was either start wearing a leash or start staying home. It was his choice."

"What did he do?" Audrey asks, taking the leash from Bradley so he can help Wyatt unload the truck.

"He'll tell you when he's ready. I'm not a snitch."

I hold the door open as they all come trooping inside.

"Hi." Wyatt smiles as he walks past, his arms loaded with wrapped up sets of long and short rods and poles and wire shelves and what must be a hundred smaller boxes of brackets and screws.

"Hi."

"Your sister put me to work," he says after he sets the armload down.

"She has a tendency to do that. It's her way."

"I'm getting that idea. Does she have you working, too?"

"She gave me the morning off with the catch that I'll be working on closets after lunch."

"Lunch smells great."

"It'll be a few minutes," Audrey says. "I'm going to put it in the oven to warm it up."

"Biscuit needs to take a walk," Wyatt says. "You want to come with?"

"Okay. Sure." I grab a jacket off one of the pegs by the back door and slide into it.

Wyatt opens the door and holds the leash tight as the dog dashes outside.

Instead of standing and watching Biscuit make his rounds, the leash requires us to walk with him.

"I feel better about him being out here with him on a leash," I say. "But what did he do?"

"It wasn't really his fault. Being from the country, he wouldn't know about traffic."

"He tried to run out in traffic?" I ask, horrified.

"Let's just say he was headed that way."

"I guess it's a good thing he had his uncle there to take care of him."

"Yeah. We had a talk. He understands."

It doesn't take long before Biscuit goes running back toward the house.

"And now he's hungry after his trip," I say.

"I didn't know I was going until your sister pushed me out the door."

"I know. She told me."

"Next time, we'll make a date of it."

"It's okay. Really." But my heart warms that he was

thinking the same thing I was thinking about how nice it would have been if I could have gone with him.

I don't want to think too much about what he and I are doing here.

I just want to enjoy it without overanalyzing it.

Thinking about it too much will take the sheen off.

Nobody said it would be easy.

THIRTY-ONE

Wyatt

AFTER LUNCH, Audrey and Bradley unwrap all the rods and poles and shelves bound together with plastic that I'd picked up in Boulder.

Audrey sits in the middle of the living room floor surrounded by white shelves of all sizes and boxes of brackets. A measuring tape in her hands. A pad of graph paper next to her.

There are also lots of long metal bars and metal shelves. Apparently, it all goes together somehow like a puzzle.

"I'm not familiar with this particular system," I say. "Does it come with directions?"

"No," Audrey says, making a check on her list and pointing for Bradley to put a stack of metal shelves off to itself. "But Lilah knows how it works."

I look at Lilah sitting calmly on the sectional, the old black cat in her lap.

"Is this true? This makes sense to you?"

"It will," she says with a little shrug. "After Audrey gets it all organized."

"It took her forever to finalize these designs," Bradley says.

"Actually this is only my closet and Audrey's. I'll do the other two closets later."

"Everything has to be exact," Lilah says.

One of the logs in the fireplace burns through, sending sparks up the chimney and Biscuit stirs in his sleep.

"It's easier than it looks," Audrey says. "I promise." She gets on her knees, tears a sheet of paper from her pad and hands it to me. "This is for Lilah's closet. That stack goes with it." She points to her left.

"And the rest of it is for your closet?"

"Lilah wanted to keep hers simple."

I smile over at Lilah. She really is the girl of my dreams.

Lilah shrugs. "I guess I'm more into painting supplies than clothes."

"I'll be right back to get the shelves." I grab the longest of the bars and head upstairs with them.

"There are screws on the coffee table," Audrey says.

I am so thankful my brother got the complicated sister. Lilah is so not complicated. And I like everything about her.

I leave the bars in her bedroom floor and head back downstairs. I meet Bradley on the stairs, headed up, his arms full.

"Having fun?" I ask.

"Actually yes. You?"

"Should be interesting."

Lilah is waiting with my drill and a box of screws.

I pick up about half the shelves. They're heavier than they look.

Lilah walks upstairs with me. "Thanks for doing this," she says. "You don't have to."

"Wouldn't miss it," I say.

She gives me a look that suggests she doesn't believe me.

After I set down the shelves and she sets down the screws and drill, I close the distance between us.

I put both my hands on either side of her face and kiss her soft lips.

"Wouldn't miss it," I whisper against her lips.

"Me either." She bites her bottom lip and looks at me with those big meadow green eyes of hers.

I kiss her again, stopping only when we hear Bradley and Audrey are coming down the hallway.

"I guess we should get busy," I whisper. "on the closet."

"I guess so." She smiles at me, her eyes glazed.

Clearing my throat, I step back. "Where do we start?" I ask, picking up a bracket. "Are you sure we're not going to accidentally build a spaceship?"

She laughs. "I think we would know that. The first step is to hang the top track."

"That's got to be this," I say, picking up the longest piece of metal.

"Yes. Now." She looks through the smaller boxes. "We need some of these long screws."

"Which way does it go?" I ask, turning it one way, then another. "The notches at the top?"

"No, Silly. The notches go at the bottom so you can slide in these other pieces."

Thinking how sexy she is when she's talking about sliding pieces into bottoms, I turn the track over and look at her. Her cheeks are a little pink and she keeps her gaze down.

"Let's do this," I say. "And hope your sister made good measurements.

"I'm sure she did. Audrey is a little bit OCD."

"I hadn't noticed," I say.

Actually I haven't noticed a whole lot of anything other than just how charming Lilah is.

If she wanted me to build a spaceship, I would figure out how to do it.

Fortunately, right now, it's a fancy closet system.

THIRTY-TWO

Lilah

THAT GRIN OF HIS—HALF trouble, half charm—spreads across Wyatt's face as he holds the level in place. "Fair warning. If I fall off this ladder, I'm blaming you."

I blink innocently. "I don't know what you're talking about."

"Right. Okay. Hand up that top rack thing."

I lift the top rack and hand up one end.

Together, we line it up with the pencil marks. Standing on a stool, I hold it steady it while he drills, the vibration humming through the wall. When the last screw goes in, I step back, a little breathless from holding it.

"That's one piece. The main piece," I say, brushing dust from my hands. "Only a hundred more to go."

"Then I hope this one is right," Wyatt says.

"Actually, we just finished the hard part. The rest of it is kind of fun."

"Good thing I'm in this for the long haul," Wyatt says, voice low as his gaze lingers on mine.

For a beat, the closet and the mess of rails and brackets don't matter at all.

My breath hitches.

In this instant, the fact that I've vowed not to get involved with anyone completely flees my head. My thinking is all focused on one thing and one thing only.

Wyatt.

He has that effect on me.

I can't help it. Couldn't help it if I wanted to.

And the thing about it is. I don't want to.

I show Wyatt how to hang the long bars and then how to attach the brackets and finally the shelves, snapping them easily in place.

"I think I've got the hang of it," he says, taking a step back to look at our handiwork.

"Yeah." I put my hands on my hips. "It looks good."

"If you sister ever needs a job, she can work as a closet designer."

"She could. That really is a thing." My brows crease.

"In Houston. I don't know if there would be much demand for it here."

"People in Whiskey Springs need closets, too."

"Maybe."

"Want help hanging your clothes up?" he asks with a little grin.

"No. I... I think I'll do it later."

I think he flustered me on purpose.

I start gathering up the packaging, putting it in a big trash bag.

"We're a good team," he says.

"Yes. I agree. We can do your closet next."

He glances at me and the words hang there as I realize what I'd just said.

"Hey," Bradley comes to the door, looking slightly frantic. "Have you seen Biscuit?"

"No," we say.

"He was in front of the fireplace when I last saw him," I tell Bradley.

"Me too."

Bradley holds up the leash. "His leash is here, but... I can't find him."

"He has to be here," Wyatt says. "We've all been up here working. No one has been outside."

"Exactly."

"Let's check," I say, moving now. "Here's Blackie. On my bed."

That's a bit unusual. The cat doesn't normally venture

upstairs.

Audrey is downstairs calling for Biscuit.

We check all the bedrooms upstairs. Just to be sure, then head down to check downstairs. Again.

I hadn't realized time had passed by so quickly. It's almost dark.

And Biscuit, large horse dog that he is, would be hard to miss.

He's not here.

THIRTY-THREE

Wyatt

BRADLEY and I grab our jackets from the pegs near the back door and flashlights before we step outside into the brisk cold air.

"How could he get outside?" I ask, knowing Bradley doesn't know any more than I do.

"Maybe the door was left cracked open."

"The cat didn't run out. The cat ran upstairs."

We look at each other. Somehow that seems significant, but I'm not sure how just yet.

"We didn't leave the doors open," I say. "We're all

hypervigilant about locking the doors, much less not leaving them open. Especially with pets."

"I know," Bradley says, running a hand through his hair. "I'm just trying to make sense of it all."

"I don't understand it either. I'm going to walk around. Check the trucks just in case."

"Okay." Bradley starts calling for his dog. Calling his name. Whistling. I can hear the strain in his voice.

I call out, too, for the dog as I walk around the side of the house, toward the trucks. I don't know how or even why Biscuit would get out to begin with, much less hop into one of our vehicles, but we're not leaving any stone unturned.

It doesn't take long for me to see that Biscuit isn't out here near the vehicles either. I walk down the road a ways, calling out, switching on my flashlight as I walk beneath the shade of the trees.

The sun is dropping behind the mountains quickly as it always does. It gets dark quick and early up here just by the nature of the position of the town and the mountains.

I walk down the dirt road, calling for Biscuit. Trying to figure out how the dog got out of the house to begin and end it all.

We were all upstairs, the four of us, working on closets. Biscuit was curled up asleep in front of the fireplace.

After the series of threatening notes that someone has been leaving at the house, I know the doors were locked.

Like I'd told Bradley, we're all careful about making sure the doors are locked. All the time.

The only explanation I can come up with chills me to the bone.

Someone let Biscuit outside.

The only tiny shred of hope I have is that he is now wearing a collar with his information on it. His name and Bradley's cell phone number.

If by chance he got out and if by chance someone finds him, they'll know who to call.

But we're so far away from any neighbors up here... that seems like an impossibility.

I shine my light out in the trees. So isolated.

Biscuit has never run off before. Before I put him on a leash... today... he always just ran around the perimeter of the yard. I don't think he's ever tried to run off. Not since Bradley got him.

Even today, when I'd pulled over at a park, he hadn't tried to run off. I was the one who had been nervous about thinking that he would. That nervousness that something would happen to him on my watch had me taking him to a pet store and outfitting him with a harness and leash and a new identification tag.

I'd thought I was helping to keep him safe.

And now this.

The wind howls through the trees, rustling the leaves on the trees. A wolf howls somewhere off in the distance.

If Biscuit is out here somewhere, I just hope he's safe.

And I hope he somehow finds his way home.

With that thought in mind, with a sudden idea, I turn around and head back to my truck. I'd heard that pets sometimes return to wherever they consider home to be.

I send my brother a quick message telling him where I'm going.

At this point, anything and everything is worth checking out.

CHAPTER
THIRTY-FOUR

Lilah

AᴜDREY SITS on the sectional in front of the fireplace staring blankly into the flames.

I pace around the room, going from window to window. Door to door.

My mind racing.

When we'd come downstairs to start looking for Biscuit, the doors had not only been closed, but they had been locked.

"There's no way he could have gotten out," I say to myself for the tenth time.

"It's all my fault," Audrey says.

"How could it possibly be your fault?" I ask, walking over and sitting next to her.

She shakes her head.

"It's this thing. With the notes and the threats. Someone wants me out of here. They're using Biscuit to get to me."

"That's crazy. How could they get inside? You changed all the door locks."

"I know." Her voice is full of misery and guilt.

I put my arms around her. "It's not your fault."

"There's no other explanation. He didn't let himself outside. And he didn't vanish into thin air. Someone had to let him out."

"But where would he go?" A little chill runs down my spine. The horse dog would not run off. I haven't seen him try to run off not even once. But that doesn't mean that he wouldn't go with someone. "There has to be an explanation."

"I know. There has to be."

"They'll find him."

"Why would someone hurt an innocent dog?" Audrey asks.

I'm not sure how to comfort her. My sister has been through so much. It hasn't even been two months since her husband died in a plane crash.

She might look like she's coping well on the outside,

but she's still grieving. In her own way. She's still grieving in her own way.

Everyone is different. But this thing with the dog has her broken up.

"Audrey," I say with all the reassurance I can muster. "They're going to find him."

She nods and take a deep breath. "They have to."

The back door opens and Bradley comes inside. Alone.

"Nothing?" I ask over my sister's head. Audrey doesn't even look up.

"Not yet. Wyatt's driving down to my cabin to look around. Just in case he got out and headed back there."

"Good idea."

I get up so Bradley can sit next to my sister and busy myself with bringing them bottles of water.

It's dark outside now. I can't imagine Biscuit being out there. Not coming when Bradley and Wyatt call him.

I start pacing again.

"What can we do?" I ask, mostly to myself.

"We wait," Bradley says.

When I hear Wyatt's truck pulling up, I step outside onto the front porch and wait while he gets out. Alone.

"No sign of him?" I ask.

"Nothing."

I walk off the porch, around the side of the house, well aware that Wyatt is right behind me.

"What do we do?" I ask.

"We wait," Wyatt says. "Come on. Let's go inside. Figure out something to eat."

"Right. Audrey's not doing well. She's got some residual stuff she's dealing with."

"It's okay." He takes my hand. Leads me back inside. Locks the doors behind us. "We can make something. We all need to eat."

CHAPTER
THIRTY-FIVE

Wyatt

Nobody ate much at dinner. Just sandwiches, but still. It's hard to get anything down when we're all worrying.

"We'll go out and start looking again in the morning," I say.

Just in case Biscuit did manage to get out, which he obviously did. And just in case he fell down the side of a cliff. We have to go look.

"I'm going to wait up," Bradley says, picking up Biscuit's leash.

"Okay."

"I'm going to wait up with him," Audrey says. Her expression looks drawn and sad.

At her core, she's still a grieving widow, even though Bradley makes her happy. She's still so vulnerable.

"I'm going to get some rest," Lilah says. "So I can get up at daybreak. Go out and help you look."

"It's the best we can do right now," I say.

I take Lilah's hand and we walk upstairs while Bradley and Audrey settle on the sectional. To wait for what, I don't know. Just to wait.

"How could this happen?" Lilah asks as we reach her room, out of earshot of Audrey and Bradley.

"I don't know," I say. "But if I find out who did this, there's going to be hell to pay."

"Too bad you don't have a decent sheriff in town to call."

"Even if we did, it wouldn't matter. Right now it's just a missing dog. Happens every day."

"But there are extenuating circumstances."

"You're right. But there's nothing we can do right now."

"I know. I just hate it."

"I do, too."

I kiss her on the forehead. "Good night, Sweetness. Try to get some sleep."

"I'll try."

"Lock your door tonight," I tell her.

She just nods, walks into her bedroom, but stops in

the doorway. "Good night, Wyatt," she says, her eyes heavy.

I nod and wait and until I hear the click of the door lock.

With a sigh, I turn around and walk into my room next door.

Although I go through the routine of getting ready for bed, brush my teeth, put on my sleep pants and a t-shirt I'd borrowed from Bradley, I doubt I'm going to actually get any sleep.

It's hard to sleep when Biscuit is missing.

I feel like I should be doing something. But the truth of the matter is, there's nothing to do.

Desperate for something to do, despite knowing there isn't anything, I drag a chair over to the window and sit down. While I sit there, waiting for the motion lights to kick on, I review the camera footage from earlier.

In our panic, not one of us thought to do that.

We have cameras all around the house, but no one thought to look at the footage.

If Biscuit went out one of the doors, he'll be on record doing it.

I take my time, starting with the front of the house, looking for any sign of the dog leaving after I got back from Boulder and we unloaded the truck.

When I don't find anything at the front of the house, I move to the camera at the back of the house.

I see myself and Wyatt walking around calling out like idiots. But no sign of the dog.

Even though I take my time, watching carefully, I don't see any sign of the dog. None.

How is it possible that a dog vanished into thin air?

CHAPTER

THIRTY-SIX

Lilah

I GET READY FOR BED. Put on my pajamas. Climb into bed.

I crawl beneath the blankets and stare into the dark at the ceiling.

As usual, my window is cracked just enough to let a little bit of fresh air in.

A wolf howls in the distance.

I shiver, worrying about Biscuit being somewhere out there.

How did he get out without anyone seeing him?

Then it hits me.

We have cameras all over the place. Watching every door from more than one angle.

I open my phone to the security camera app and scroll back to where Wyatt and I had taken Biscuit for a walk out back.

From there, I watch the footage. If Biscuit went out, he'll be on camera.

I watch until my eyes get heavy.

I get up. Walk around. Then watch the footage until I see Wyatt and Bradley walking around looking and calling for Biscuit.

No sign of the big dog in between.

I switch over to the front of the house. Do the same thing.

I watch until my eyes hurt.

No sign of him getting out.

How is that possible?

It's not possible. Does that mean that the dog is somewhere in the house?

Getting up, I put on my shoes and walk downstairs.

The house is quiet. Too quiet.

Bradley and Audrey are curled up asleep on the sectional. Blackie asleep in the big comfortable chair.

I walk around. Checking doors first.

I honestly don't see any place that a big dog could hide. Not that he would. Biscuit is a social dog not prone to hiding. I can't see him hiding unless he were to get sick.

But we've looked everywhere.

The window shades are down. Comforting.

I walk to the front door. Look out.

Then walk to the back door and look out.

The only thing I see is a bird flying about.

Then I hear something scratching at the front door.

Hurrying to the door, I look out.

I see… a tail wagging.

A tail?

Then I hear a dog bark. A single familiar bark.

"Biscuit?"

I unlock the door.

Just as I unlock the door, I hear Wyatt bounding down the stairs.

"What are you doing?" Wyatt calls out, breathless.

I open the door and Biscuit rushes inside, wiggling all over.

Audrey and Bradley stir from their place on the sectional.

"It's Biscuit," I say, kneeling down to put my arms around the dog wiggling in ten different directions at once.

Biscuit licks my face and I let him. God help me, I let him.

I hadn't known just how attached I'd gotten to this big gangly dog.

Then Bradley and Audrey are there.

Audrey wraps her arms around the dog, tears dampening his fur.

Bradley checks him out. Looking him over from head to toe. No broken bones or scuffs or anything noticeable.

Wyatt steps out front to look for any sign of anyone who might have walked or driven up.

I follow. "He just wanders back up?" I ask.

"I don't know. He's doesn't look like he's been outside. His feet aren't muddy."

"What the heck?" I ask, looking at Wyatt.

He shakes his head.

Bradley sticks his head out the door. "Hey. You've got to see this."

There's a piece of paper, an envelope maybe, crudely taped onto his collar with packing tape.

After Bradley takes a photo of it, for evidence, Audrey cuts it off with scissors.

With trembling hands, she pulls the note folded up out of an also folded envelope and smooths it out.

"What does it say?" I ask.

After reading the note, Audrey hands the paper to Bradley who then hands it to Wyatt who finally hands it to me.

It's a handwritten note.

One line.

And it makes my blood run cold.

Are you sure you want to live here?

THIRTY-SEVEN

Wyatt

I'D ALWAYS figured Midnight was a good time to have a beer.

Tonight is no exception.

We offered Biscuit food, but he's not hungry. Whoever *borrowed* him must have fed him. Have I seen stranger things? Maybe. Maybe not.

I'm reserving that designation until I have more information.

All four of us, Bradley, Audrey, Lilah, and me, sit on the sectional in front of the fireplace. All of us watching

Biscuit sleep. He's the only one of us who doesn't appear to be disturbed about being gone for several hours.

All of us, even Lilah, hold a bottle of cold beer in our hands.

The note lies on the coffee table like a harbinger. A vile harbinger that no one wants to touch now that we know what it is.

Audrey pulls her feet up under her and rests her head on Bradley's shoulder.

"How did he get past the cameras?" Lilah asks.

I reach over and take her hand in mine. "We missed something. That's all."

"And the driveway. We didn't get any alerts on the driveway. He had to have driven up here, took Biscuit, left with him. Then came back with him."

"Maybe he didn't drive," Bradley says.

We all just look at him. Too drained to process anything complicated.

"It's possible he dodged the cameras."

"He would have to know where they are." Lilah picks up her phone. Stares at the blank screen. "Where the blind spots are."

"I don't think we have any blind spots," Bradley says.

"There are always blind spots," I say, rubbing my thumb in little circles on Lilah's palm. "And I say that as the one who installed them. Making every endeavor to avoid blind spots."

"We missed it," Lilah says in my defense.

"We'll go back through all the footage. On all the cameras," Bradley says.

"Biscuit's sleeping in my room tonight," Audrey says, sleepily.

"Blackie, too," Lilah says, scratching the old cat's ears. He starts purring and turns over on his side, stretching out his paws.

I squeeze her hand.

"We go into hypervigilant mode," I say.

"No ladies or pets are to be left alone for any reason," Bradley declares.

I expect blowback from that statement, but we don't get any. All I can guess is that Lilah and Audrey are too tired or too shell-shocked from the whole night's ordeal to protest.

"Okay," Audrey murmurs.

"Yeah," Lilah says simply.

"When do you want to get started on going through the footage?" I ask Bradley.

"First thing in the morning. Need to get Audrey up to bed." Audrey lifts her head. "And I need to take Biscuit out for a quick walk."

"His definition of quick is different from everyone else's," I say. "I'll take him."

"Then I'm coming with you," Lilah says, looking at me with defiance. There's some of blowback I'd been expecting.

"I'll check the doors," Bradley says. "Drop the cat off in Lilah's room."

I stand up, pulling Lilah up with me. "Good plan." I pick up Biscuit's leash. "Come on, Boy. Looks like you're going to be wearing this thing permanently for awhile."

Biscuit stands up. Shakes off the sleep. I clip the leash onto his harness.

"Weird timing," Lilah says. "On the whole leash thing."

"A bit."

While Bradley heads upstairs with Blackie on one arm and Audrey on the other, we put on our coats and go outside, keeping Biscuit on a short leash.

We don't talk. I keep a firm grip on her hand as though someone might whisk her away if I so much as lose sight of her for less than an instant.

As we follow Biscuit around the perimeter, we both stay alert, looking around.

The reality of it is that whoever stole Biscuit is probably more than long gone.

It doesn't matter. The damage is done.

The full moon hangs low over the snow-capped mountains peaks, casting a glow over the white caps.

Biscuit doesn't seem to need his usual long length of time to do his business. It's almost as though he knows it's not his usual time to be outside. He scratches his back legs, throwing leaves into the air before heading toward the back door.

"I guess it's time for us to go back inside," I say.

"Not a minute too soon," Lilah says with one more glance around toward the darkness created by the tree line.

THIRTY-EIGHT

Lilah

EVEN THOUGH BRADLEY already checked the doors, Wyatt checks them again before we go upstairs. Makes sure the fire is banked for the night.

Biscuit gallops up the stairs without protest. It almost seems like he knows he's not spending the rest of the night downstairs.

"He doesn't seem to mind," Wyatt says as we reach the top of the stairs and turn toward Audrey's bedroom.

"Maybe he knows she has a fireplace in her room."

"Does she?" he asks, surprised.

"She does. I can't wait until she gives in and installs heated floors."

"Bradley and I can install those," he says without a hitch.

"Well," I say. "That's handy."

"We do come in handy on occasion."

Bradley is waiting at Audrey's door for his dog.

"Here he is," Wyatt says. "All ready for the night."

Biscuit runs straight for the fireplace and lies down on the rug someone put there for him.

"That dog might be a little bit spoiled," I say after we tell them goodnight and walk down the hallway toward my room.

"I didn't hear you complaining when he was licking your face."

"You weren't supposed to see that," I say. "I can't stand the thought of someone hurting an animal."

I open my door and peek inside to see Blackie asleep on the foot of my bed.

"Do you have to go already? Or can you stay a little while?"

"I can stay."

"Good." I smile. I'm not ready to be alone.

He follows me into the bedroom and closes the door behind us.

"I wanted to talk to you anyway."

"Oh? What about?" I sit on the comfortable chair in the sitting area of my room.

"I'm worried about you being here."

"I'm not by myself."

"I know." He rubs the back of his neck. "As we saw tonight, that doesn't matter, does it?"

"I suppose not." Closing my eyes, I lean back in the chair. "I'm just relieved that Biscuit is okay."

"It's an offense to steal someone's dog. It's a felony here in Colorado. Class four. Up to six years prison time."

"I'm surprised you know that," I say, untying my boots and pulling my feet up under me.

"I have a fount of useless information in my head."

"Doesn't seem so useless to me. Now all we have to do is find out who did it."

"Harder than it seems."

"Is that what you wanted to tell me?" I ask, opening my eyes.

"No. I wanted to talk to you about staying with me at my cabin until this is resolved. Or if you don't want to do that, staying with my parents."

"Oh." I take a breath. That's not what I expected. Not that I had any expectations. "I can't leave my sister here alone."

"I had a feeling you were going to say that," he says, dropping onto the ottoman in front of the chair.

"You knew I would."

He takes my hand, clasps his fingers with mine. "In that case, I hope you don't mind me staying here."

"You've already got your own room," I say, trying to

keep the smile off my face. I like the idea of him staying here. "I don't mind."

"Good." He brushes a thumb over my knuckles. "Because I'm not letting you out of my sight until we get this sorted out."

"Then I guess we should spend some time tomorrow measuring and designing your closet."

"Looks like it." He looks at me with his blue eyes that remind me of a clear summer day.

He scoops me up and sits snuggled next to me in the comfortable chair.

I'm beginning to understand my sister a little better. How she's come up here and fallen in love in the high altitude with its clean air.

"So this is how it happens," I say, my voice muffled against his shoulder.

"What's that?"

"Nothing. Nothing at all."

I tilt my head up and he kisses me.

But it's not nothing, I realize.

It's everything.

CHAPTER
THIRTY-NINE

Wyatt

THE FOUR OF us spend the next morning going through all the recorded camera footage together. We put it on the television and sit on the sectional. Surely one of four sets of eyes will catch anything, however subtle.

Bradley and Audrey sitting side by side.

Lilah snuggled next to me.

Biscuit is in his place in front of the fireplace and Blackie is asleep on his end of the sectional.

As intent and methodical as we are in watching every minute of every camera, we don't see anything.

Just as we're finishing up, I get a call to go out to one of the cabins to fix a broken toilet.

Lilah walks me to the door.

"I know it sounds silly, but no one stays alone," I tell her. "Okay?"

"You don't have to worry about that. I'm on board."

"Good." He turns at the sound of a vehicle coming up the road. "The mail is here."

The mailman stops in front of the house and brings a box along with the mail to the door.

"Everything going good?" the mailman asks.

"As good as can be expected," I say.

"This one is mine," Lilah says, taking the box.

"What did you get?"

"Just some office supplies," she says with a little shrug.

The mailman gets back in his jeep and drives back down the road.

I watch him leave.

"You're wondering if he did it," she says.

"He wouldn't have any reason to do it."

"Not that we know of. I don't think we can rule anyone out right now."

"I'm missing something and I can't figure out what it is," I say.

"You'll think of it. Go. I'll be here when you get back."

"I'm counting on it."

I pull her into my arms and kiss her. I know she's not here alone. I know my brother is here and her sister.

But still. I don't like leaving her.

"We'll be okay," she says.

"I'm counting on it. Call me if you need me. If anything doesn't feel right. Anything at all."

"Don't worry." She smiles. You'll be right back."

As I walk to my truck, I realize that I will be right back.

And this is exactly where I want to be.

I want to be where Lilah is.

I'd known it all along. Since the moment I first saw her.

But this is different. This is a deeper feeling.

She stands there on the front porch, holding her box, watching me.

Before I back out, I lower my window. "Lock the door."

With a shrug, she opens the door and disappears inside.

I know exactly what she's thinking and I hate it that I'm thinking the same thing.

Locking the door doesn't change anything.

Someone is able to get inside anyway.

If I believed in ghosts, I would be thinking it was something ghostly.

I don't not believe in ghosts, but either way I don't believe ghosts are the ones leaving threatening notes and stealing a dog away for hours just to bring him back with, of course, a threatening note.

As I drive down the road, past the hidden security cameras, I can't shake the feeling that I'm missing something.

I'll figure it out.

One way or another, we're going to put a stop to this nonsense.

CHAPTER

FORTY

Lilah

WHILE AUDREY and Bradley install more of the motorized window shades, I make myself a mug of hot tea. So many windows. So many beautiful views. But at night, those beautiful windows give anyone outside a front row seat to whatever we're doing inside.

With my hot tea, I sit down at the kitchen table and sort through my new office supplies. It's not much. Just markers and index cards. Medium poster sized index cards and smaller index cards.

It's not much, but when I look at it, I see a world of possibilities before me.

Blackie comes over and, climbing up on the table, lays down to watch me work.

I reach over and scratch his head, then open my laptop and get started.

Despite the threats that loom over us at every turn, being here with my sister and her boyfriend feels cozy and comfortable.

I find myself wondering if our sister, Brianna, would like it here. I can't really picture her here, though. She's a city girl through and through.

And I wonder what she would think about the notes and the threats.

She'd probably have it figured out already.

Brianna is probably the smartest of the three of us. She's a paralegal and a personal assistant, and can do any office job put in front of her.

I think that's why she likes doing temp work. Not only does she like a challenge, but she would have trouble picking just what it is that she likes best.

"You look deep in thought," Audrey says, coming over for a drink of water.

"I'm taking Biscuit out for a walk," Bradley says. Then adds over his shoulder. "Don't go anywhere."

"We'll be right here," Audrey assures him, sitting down next to me. "I'm not even going to ask what it is you're doing," she say, glancing at my stacks of index cards.

"Good. Because I don't even know myself."

She narrows her eyes at me. "This reminds me of when you started bartending." She holds up a hand and looks away. "But I'm not asking. I don't need to know."

I smile. It's nice to be understood without judgement. Something only a close sister can do.

I sit back in my chair and tap a marker on the table. "Do you think we'll figure out who's doing these things?"

"Yes," she says without hesitation. "With the four of us putting our heads together, we'll figure it out."

"I still think we need to tell the guys about the money. They need to know just how high the stakes are."

"You're right. I know you're right." She leans her elbows on the table and watches Bradley walking Biscuit out back. "Do you really think it would change anything?"

I wonder how she means it. "I don't think Bradley would see you any differently."

"I guess I worry that he'll think I'm just here for the money."

"Really? I hadn't considered it that way. Audrey. I said this all along and I still believe it. I think you'd be a fool to not at least give living here a try. And that's what you did." I follow her gaze out back. I understand her not wanting to upset things that are going well. "You do like it here, don't you?"

"I do. It's funny. I haven't gotten out much. Only been into town a handful of times. But I don't mind. It's peaceful here."

"Do you think you'll get cabin fever?" I ask. "Especially with winter coming up?"

"I guess we'll find out. But I don't think so."

I wonder how much of that has to do with Bradley. But I don't ask her. Not right now. That's a conversation for another day.

At the sound of a vehicle coming up the driveway, we both look at each other.

"Wyatt's back," I say. And my heart does funny little flip.

"Go let him in," Audrey says.

"Right. He doesn't have a key."

"Let me know if we need to fix that," Audrey says as I head toward the door.

I give her a look over my shoulder. But she knows.

She knows I like Wyatt.

I'm not sure I want her to know just how much.

Maybe I should start admitting that how much I like him to myself first.

FORTY-ONE

Wyatt

I PULL up to Audrey's house and park.

Before getting out, I grab the flower on the passenger seat. It wasn't a rose this time. Just a bright, happy yellow wildflower.

I hadn't bothered to go by the General Store and I hadn't wanted to stop by John's backyard, so I just stopped and cut a flower in a meadow on the side of the road. It was on our property, so no harm done.

Lilah appears at the front door.

I could get used to coming home and having my woman waiting for me.

"Hi," I say, leaning forward to give her a kiss.

"Hi." She smiles.

"I brought you something." I hold up the yellow wild-flower. "Nothing fancy. Just a wildflower."

Her face lights up. "It's a daisy." She twirls it in her hand and gives me a smug look. "Some people call it the old man of the mountain."

"That's odd."

"I can tell you more, but I'm not sure you want to know."

We step inside and lock the door behind us. Bradley is getting ready to go back up the ladder to continue installing the window shades. Biscuit is settling down in front of the fireplace. I assume they just got back inside from Biscuit's walk.

"Now you have to tell me."

"Well," she says, running a hand over the petals of the flower. "If I'm right. It takes 12-20 years to grow before it flowers just one time. Then it dies."

I feel the blood drain from my face. "Twenty years? That flower is twenty years old?"

"Maybe. I'll put it in some water."

"You're right. I didn't want to know that. I thought it was just a wildflower."

"It is. Now we get to enjoy it." She kisses me on the cheek before she places it in a vase full of water. "Thank you."

"No excitement while I was gone?" I ask, not wanting

to think about how I'd just randomly picked a flower that took twenty-years to bloom.

"No. It's been calm. Peaceful."

Blackie hops up onto the island and meows at her.

She opens a can of food and puts some on a plate for him.

I grab a bottle of water and go to the dining table where someone has been working.

Since Audrey and Bradley are doing their thing, I assume that person to be Lilah.

"What are you working on?" I ask, sitting down in front of the laptop computer where the screensaver is blocking her screen.

"Nothing," she says quickly. Too quickly.

While she pours some dry cat food in a bowl, I tap the keyboard, but the screen is locked.

Not my business anyway.

I pick up the top card from one of several stacks of index cards on the table.

"What's a pasque flower?" I ask.

She looks at me sideways, obviously debating on how to answer. "It's a member of the buttercup family. Also called the April Fool flower. It blooms in April, then usually gets snowed over and disappears."

"These flowers live a harsh and dangerous life."

I pick up another card. It has another flower name written on it.

With the card in my hand, I lean back in the chair and grin like a loon at her.

"You're studying flowers," I say.

She comes to stand next to me. Closes the lid on her computer.

"I was just playing around. I wanted to see just how much work you had ahead of you. In case you decided you wanted to go forward with your flower shop idea."

I pull her into my lap."

She laughs nervously, glancing toward her sister. I kiss her on the cheek.

"I see," I say. "Looks like you put in a lot of work while you were playing around."

"It kept me looking busy so I didn't have to help hang window shades."

"Smart girl. Want to help me cook pasta for dinner?"

"Okay. Sure."

And then she and I have some things to talk about. She's gone and done it now. I was on the fence about the whole flower shop thing. A lot of it hinged on her. I wasn't about to try doing it on my own. But with both of us working on it... that gives it a whole new life.

And, quite honestly, it gives me a whole new perspective on a lot of things, not the least of which is Lilah.

FORTY-TWO

Lilah

"WANT to hear something funny about Bradley?" Wyatt asks as I boil water for the pasta.

"Always."

"He was convinced that if he could teach me and Caleb how to make spaghetti, we could use it to impress girls."

"That's kind of sweet."

"Yes, but..." Wyatt lowers his voice. "Our grandmother in Boston taught him how to cook it."

"What's wrong with that?" I turn on the heat under the pot of water.

"No spices. None. Blandest spaghetti ever."

The sound of Bradley's drill drowns out his words.

"I haven't heard Audrey complaining."

"She wouldn't. Besides, she doesn't count."

"She counts. She's from Houston. She knows good food."

"Don't doubt that. Still. She would like it because he made it. Anyway. I stopped by my cabin and cut some fresh basil and oregano. Makes all the difference."

"I'm looking forward to it. Are you making homemade sauce?" And the man grows his own herbs. This is getting more interesting by the moment.

"Of course. Even though I have to admit, when it's just me, I sometimes open a jar. Spice it up."

"Nothing wrong with opening a jar."

"I know, right? We'll do that next time."

"Okay." Every time he says something like *next time*, I get all giddy inside. Saying *next time* implies that we'll be doing something again. In the future.

I decide to push it a little. Just to see what he says.

"Maybe after all this threatening business is over with."

"Yes. After things settle down."

I go into the pantry and pull out a couple of cans of black olives.

"You put black olives in your spaghetti?" he asks.

"Of course. Don't you?"

"I guess I do now."

"It's not good without black olives," I say, finding a can opener in one of the drawers.

"Let me get that," he says, taking the can opener. "Do you chop these up or put them in whole?"

"I chop them."

"Okay." He gets out a cutting board and knife.

"So did it work?" I ask.

"Did what work?"

"Did it impress girls?"

"I don't know. I never tried it."

I stop and look at him. "I guess I'll let you know."

"I'm not sure this one counts. You added black olives to my recipe."

"Only to make it better," I say. "I think it counts."

"If you want it to count, it counts."

I smile. "You use fresh tomatoes?"

"Of course."

I stand with hands on the counter behind me, watching him slice tomatoes on a cutting board. He's handy. He can wield a kitchen knife as deftly as he can wield an axe. So many layers to this man. And I'd like to learn them all.

It wasn't a rose this time. Just a bright, happy yellow wildflower. But Wyatt had brought me a flower. And that means something in anyone's book.

It definitely means something in my book. It tells me I might not be alone in this growing affection that I'm feeling.

CHAPTER

FORTY-THREE

Wyatt

LILAH TEARS LETTUCE for a salad as I chop tomatoes and black olives for the spaghetti sauce.

I smile when I catch her watching me and she looks away quickly.

She's complicated, this Lilah.

She can put together the pieces of a complicated closet without a hitch. She can paint a scene that makes a man think he's looking out a window. And she isn't the least bit afraid to learn anything.

She went from knowing nothing about alcohol to

being a bartender. And now she's going from knowing nothing about flowers to learning them.

She's impressive enough to take a man's breath away.

"So if Bradley didn't teach you how to make spaghetti sauce, how did you learn?" she asks.

"I took what he showed me and figured out how to make it better."

"So you're basically self-taught."

"I guess you could say that." I pick up a wooden spoon and stir the tomato sauce in the pot.

"We're a lot alike in that," she says. "Are you not close to your other brother?"

"Caleb? Yeah. We're all close. Caleb is just different. He travels a lot."

"I thought he took care of the family business."

"He does. But has other ventures, too. He likes Whiskey Springs, but I think it would stifle him if he had to stay here all the time."

"He sounds like our sister, Brianna. She can't stand to stay in the same job for too long. More than a couple of weeks and she gets antsy."

"How can she change jobs every ten weeks?" He looks at me in confusion. "Does she work for herself?"

"No. But she should. She does temp work for different agencies."

"Oh. What was it like growing up with two sisters?"

"We were two years apart, so we didn't have to compete. We had completely different social groups."

"Yeah. You don't really get that privilege in a small town. Everybody knows everybody and we were all right there together even though we were in different grades."

"I can't imagine. Can I have one of your tomatoes for the salad?"

"Sure. Catch." He holds up the tomato and makes as though he's going to toss it to me like a football.

"Oh no." She holds up a hand. "You do not want to do that. I'm not good at sports." She glances over her shoulder. "Audrey will kill me for making a mess."

I step over and gently place the tomato in her hand. "Have I stumbled upon something you're not good at?"

"Maybe," she says, setting the tomato on her own cutting board.

"Hard to believe. So if you didn't play sports growing up, what did you do?"

"Guess. What do you think I did?"

"Hmm." I put a hand on my chin and study her. "Something in the spotlight, but not too much. Not a cheerleader."

She watches me with amusement.

"Majorette," I say. "That's definitely it."

"Close enough. I actually did a couple of majorette parade things, but color guard."

"Color guard? The flags?"

"That's right. I can twirl a flag like you wouldn't believe."

"It suits you," I say. "With the colors and the movement."

"You think so?"

"Yes. You're not flashy. You're artistic. And you're too pretty to be hidden in a band uniform."

"Audrey was in the band. Don't tell her that."

"I won't. So your other sister, let me guess. Cheerleader."

"How did you know that?" she asks, looking truly baffled. "You haven't even met Brianna."

"Just from what you've said about her."

"Very little," she says, her brows knitted.

"Would you believe I played football?" I ask to distract her away from my uncanny ability to figure out what people are good at.

Now she's studying me. "You don't look like a football player."

I put a hand over my heart. "Now you've wounded me."

She laughs. "I meant that as a compliment."

"You do know I'm a guy, right?"

"I am well aware. Quarterback?"

"What gave me away?"

She shrugs prettily. "I can't tell you that."

Lilah Sinclair has tested my resolve since the moment I first saw her.

"I—"

Bradley walks by, interrupting whatever I was going

to say. "We're taking Biscuit out for a quick walk," he says.

I notice that Biscuit is on his leash.

"No hurry," I say. "It'll be awhile before dinner is ready."

After Audrey and Bradley are outside, I pick Lilah up by the waist and set her on the island counter.

"You're driving me crazy with wanting to kiss you," I say just before I place my lips on hers.

We kiss until we hear my brother and Audrey coming back to the door, talking to each other. I slide her off the counter and we both, for all appearances, go back to what we were doing.

Lilah has somehow placed a spell on me.

I simply can't get enough of her.

FORTY-FOUR

Lilah

"It's a pretty night," Bradley says after dinner, while we're still sitting at the table.

"It doesn't seem as cold tonight," I say.

"Want to go outside? Sit on the porch swing?"

"Is that allowed?" I glance over at my sister.

"We agreed that no one would be left alone," she says. "We didn't agree that we'd be prisoners in our own home."

"Good point," I murmur. "Okay. Sure."

"You two cooked," Bradley says. "We'll clean up. Go on."

We put on our jackets and step outside, the motion light clicking on. It might not be as cold, but it's definitely cooler than what I'm used to back in Houston.

We sit on the swing and wait for the motion light to cycle off.

"It feels like we're doing something dangerous," I say.

"We probably are."

I look over sharply at Wyatt, but he doesn't look the least bit concerned. He looks relaxed.

I pull my jacket tighter.

"Cold?" he asks.

"A little."

He scoots closer and puts an arm around me. We sit still. Waiting for the light to click off.

I can't help wondering if we're being watched. Wondering when the next note will appear somewhere.

The light clicks off, leaving us in darkness. It takes a minute for my eyes to adjust.

"It's peaceful out here," Wyatt says.

"I guess so."

"Close your eyes. Listen."

I close my eyes. I hear the river rumbling in the distance. The eerie sound of a wolf somewhere hopefully far away. The television playing inside the house.

"It is peaceful," I admit. "I just hate that someone is trying to take that away."

"We won't let him." He kisses the top of my head. "I wanted to talk to you."

"What every girl wants to hear."

"Not like that. This is a good thing. Hopefully. I hope you'll like it."

I can't help holding my breath. He'd said he would stay here until the stalker is stopped. I don't want him to move out. His being here is one of the things I like most about living here.

"I've been thinking about the flower shop."

"Oh." I should have known that was what he wanted to talk about. "What are you thinking?"

"Do you think it's something you'd like to take on? With me?"

"I can help you get started. I've already started learning basic flower things. I know there's a ton more. Soil. And light. And how to water. And what's popular."

"I know. But not like that. I mean a partnership. We go in 50-50."

Again. Not what I was expecting.

"Why?" I ask.

He doesn't answer right away.

The wind rustles in the aspen leaves and an owl makes his presence known with loud hoots.

"I have several reasons," he says.

"Like?"

"First of all, I think you'd be good at it. I've got the capital and you've got the brains."

This comes as a surprise to me. I know that his family owns their own business but that doesn't always mean they have working capital for other things.

"I don't have any money," I say.

"Like I said. I've got the money." He takes my hand and laces his fingers with mine.

"Who would run it?" I ask.

"We would."

"You've got your family business."

"I can do both. Actually my part is pretty small."

"Where?" I ask.

"That's the part I don't have figured out yet. There's a vacant building in town. We could check that out. See if there's room behind that building for a greenhouse."

"What's the other option?"

"We'd have to talk to Audrey, but we could put it here."

"Here? Where?"

"I'm thinking somewhere walking distance of the house."

"Do you think people would drive up here? For flowers?"

"I do think so. It's not that far. But. We'd build a website so most of our work would be deliveries."

"Or special events. Like weddings."

"Yes. And the lodge is always having some kind of function. We could market to them. Save them from having to drive in to Boulder to pick up flowers. They might even use more flowers if they have somewhere local to shop."

"You've really thought a lot about this."

"I guess I have."

"I thought the idea just occurred to you. What? A couple of days ago?"

He looks into my eyes. "When I figure something out, I don't like to waste time."

I wonder if we're still talking about the flower shop now.

"I was hoping to get some painting done," I say, but I have a sinking feeling that my painting just took another back seat.

"You can do both. I'm not asking you to give up anything." He looks away. "Maybe it was a bad idea."

"No," I say. "It's a good idea. And if we can do it here, it's an even better idea."

"Think about it then," he says. "Take your time. There's no need to rush into it."

"Maybe we should talk to Audrey and Bradley. See what they think."

"I think we should. You're freezing. Let's go inside."

"Good idea." I'm up before he is and the motion light clicks on.

He's right behind me and seconds later, we're back inside the warm house.

I'm not sure if I'll ever get used to the cold weather. Not completely anyway.

But I'm pretty sure I'm getting used to being with Wyatt.

Now I have to figure out if I can take a commitment as big as helping him open a flower shop when I could be summoned back to Houston at any time.

I already know I can't put him off for two years while I wait to see what my future holds.

Wyatt isn't the kind of man who waits for anything.

FORTY-FIVE

Wyatt

I GET up before daylight the next morning to find my brother already up making coffee.

"Morning," I say. "What are you doing up so early?"

"Biscuit needed a walk." He hands me a mug of coffee, then makes another one for himself.

"Good reason. I guess."

"He thought so."

"Did we make it through the night without incident?"

"It appears so."

"Any new ideas on how to put a stop to it?"

"We can do the stakeout again."

"We can." Something occurs to me. "Trent."

"What?"

I've got a friend in Boulder. His name is Trent. I can drive down. See what he thinks about the videos. See if we're missing something."

"Okay." He sits at the table. Notices Lilah's index cards. "What's all this?"

"Just a project Lilah and I are playing around with."

"Flowers?"

"There's no flower shop in town."

"Needs to be."

"I know." Somehow hearing my brother validate my crazy idea makes me feel less crazy.

"Thinking you'd put one in town?"

"Maybe. Or up here."

"Hmm. Might be a challenge in winter. Getting deliveries into town."

"At least we'd be here when the weather gets bad. Instead of being obligated to drive in to town. And to keep an eye on things."

"Yeah. I guess you could use one of those drones to deliver them down to town."

"A drone. Sometimes you're brilliant."

"I was just kidding."

"Right. But it's not a bad idea. I don't know how it would work. But it has possibilities."

"You think on it, Bro. Let me know when you're going in to Boulder to talk to your friend."

"I will," I say.

"The flower shop's a good idea. Especially with Lilah helping. Audrey says Lilah's memory is crazy good."

"We'd be partners," I say.

"I would expect so. That's how it usually works when you're married."

I don't say anything.

"Getting cold feet yet?" he asks, taunting me.

"Not going to. Wondering why you're dragging yours though."

"I don't move as fast as you do."

"You like her, right?"

"You know I like her."

"Okay. You'll figure it out."

We both sit quietly sipping our coffee.

"Is it weird us living here together?" I ask.

"Not to me. Now if Caleb lived here, too, that would be weird."

I laugh. "I have to agree with you."

"I'm going to take Audrey coffee in bed."

"That's a sweet gesture."

"I'm a sweet guy."

"Who needs to figure out his next move."

"My next move is taking Audrey coffee." He gets up and starts making coffee.

"Good God, Man. You move slow."

"Shut up."

I grin. Things are going well. It's early, but I go ahead

and text my friend. See if he has time to look at the videos on my phone apps today.

He answers immediately.

"Don't have to go in to Boulder. He can log in and look at our camera footage remotely."

"It's the world we live in, Bro."

"Yes. It is."

"I'll see you in a bit," he says. "Try to stay out of trouble."

Laughing, I take a sip of coffee, then give Trent a call so he can help me figure out how to get him into our cameras.

I'm good at installing them in the right places, but I'm missing something. If anybody can figure it out, it's my buddy Trent.

CHAPTER

FORTY-SIX

Lilah

WHEN I GET DOWNSTAIRS, the next morning, Wyatt is sitting at the kitchen table, with the iPad we use for the security cameras.

He's talking to someone on the phone.

"Good morning," he says, looking up.

"Good morning."

"Call me if you figure anything out. I've got to go make breakfast for my girl."

I stop, almost to the kitchen. Blackie winds around my legs and I absently pick him up, running my hands through his fur.

For just a second, there's a hitch in my thoughts. I wonder who he's going to make breakfast for.

Then I realize he's talking about me.

"Want a bacon, egg, and cheese sandwich?" he asks.

"Sure." *My girl.* He told someone on the phone that I'm his girl.

While he's pulling everything out of the refrigerator, eggs, bacon, cheese, I fill Blackie's food bowl.

"Everything okay?" I ask, my hands shaking a little bit.

"Yes." He cracks an egg into a bowl and looks at me. "I made an executive decision. I hope you're okay with it."

"Me?"

"Yeah. Maybe I should have asked Audrey. Either way." He goes back to the refrigerator for milk.

"What kind of decision?" I slide onto a barstool.

"I have a buddy in Boulder. We went to college together. He's a genius when it comes to technology."

"Okay."

"I gave him the password to your security cameras."

"Why?" I ask slowly, trying to figure out what he's thinking.

He whips the egg and milk together in the bowl while he watches me.

"Because I'm missing something and I can't figure out what it is. If anybody can figure it out, Trent can."

"Okay," I say with a shrug.

He smiles.

"I trust you Wyatt. I don't think you'd do anything to put us in any kind of danger."

He dumps the egg mixture in the skillet. Adds some spices. "I'm doing everything I can to keep you safe."

"I know. So what did he say?"

"He's going to need a little time to take a look. He's got to work today, so it might be this weekend before he gets to it. But knowing Trent, he won't be able to resist working on it."

"You told him what's going on?"

"More or less. That someone is getting past the cameras." He puts bacon in a skillet on the stove.

"It's really strange, isn't it?" Then. "Where is everybody?"

"They're upstairs planning Bradley's closet."

"I see."

"Yeah. I don't think it's really for Bradley though."

"How long do you think they'll pretend that it's his room?"

Wyatt laughs. "My brother is a little slow sometimes."

"He's not slow," I say. "He's being respectful of Audrey's newly widowed state."

"Right. You're right." He turns the bacon. Stirs the eggs.

Resting my chin on my hands, I think back over my conversation with Audrey. About how she needs to tell the guys about her inheritance. It's relevant. It would let them know just how high the stakes are. A motivation for someone wanting us out of the house.

Maybe I need to be open with Wyatt. Maybe I need to tell him why I shouldn't get too close to him.

"I need to tell you something," I say.

"Okay," he says, buttering four pieces of bread.

But I don't want to tell him. I REALLY don't want to tell him. I don't want him to think less of me. I don't want him to know that I'm anything other than who he thinks I am.

Not someone who could be going to jail.

He deserves better than that.

"What do you want to tell me?"

"The reason I'm here," I say. I'll start off slow. Start with the easy stuff, then work up to the harder stuff.

He puts a sandwich on a plate. Slides it over to me.

Then comes around with his own.

"Coffee," he says. "I forgot your coffee."

"No." I put a hand on his arm. "I'll get some orange juice, then drink coffee after I eat."

"I'll get it." He's up, getting me a glass of orange juice.

"Be careful," I say. "I could get used to this."

"That's my plan."

I smile, but on the inside, I'm groaning. I can't do it. I can't tell him. Not right now.

Maybe I'll tell him later.

I love the way he looks at me. I don't want to do anything to jeopardize that.

Not yet.

I can't let him think I'm some kind of person who could go to jail. Even if it wasn't really my fault. Even if I was provoked.

The conversation shifts back to Audrey and Bradley and my statement about telling him why I'm here falls aside, lost in the air waves.

I left it drift away. Another day.

I'll bring it up again another time.

Maybe after this whole stalking thing is sorted out. Right now there's just too much going on to complicate things.

Guys don't like things that are too complicated and I don't want to run him off.

I want to keep him.

"This is good," I say. "Why do guys always know how to make eggs."

"Didn't you know? They teach that in *How to Treat a Girl Right 101*." He says it with such a straight face, a laugh bubbles up before I can stop it.

FORTY-SEVEN

Wyatt

WHILE LILAH RESEARCHES flowers and makes index cards, stopping to go back over them now and them. Telling me little things about them, I research greenhouses.

"It's like learning a foreign language," she says. "Just linking things together. Like this daisy. It's called the old man of the mountain because the petals look sort of like beards. So I picture a daisy with a beard."

I glance at the yellow daisy on the table in front of us. "I'll never look at daisies the same way again."

"Don't think about it like that. Just be silly with it. The sillier the better."

When the doorbell rings, Lilah nearly jumps out of her skin and I'm not much better off.

Before we even have time to react, Audrey and Bradley are coming down the stairs.

"Who's at the door?" Audrey asks.

"I don't know," Lilah say.

"I'll get it," Bradley says.

"I don't think our guy is going to come up and ring the doorbell," Wyatt says.

"I agree," Lilah says. "That's a good point."

Bradley opens the door and Claire is standing there.

"Claire. Come in."

Claire steps inside. "I hope I'm not intruding. It smells so good in here. Like a coffee shop." She glances over at us, wringing her hands nervously. "The sheriff told me you were keeping Blackie and I—"

Blackie jumps down from where he'd been sitting on the sectional and runs over to her.

"There you are," she say, scooping him up.

I can hear him purring all the way over here.

"She's going to take him home," Lilah says. "I'll gather up his things." She proceeds to start gathering up all Blackie's food and putting it in a tote bag.

"How are you, Claire?" Audrey asks, putting a hand on Claire's arm. "You've been through so much."

"You probably don't want me here," Claire says. "I hope you believe me when I say I'm not the one who left notes at your door."

"I know that," Audrey says. "I'm so sorry you got accused like that."

"Well. It's water under the bridge now," Claire says with a nervous smile.

"Are you okay?" I ask Lilah, speaking softly so only she can hear.

"Yes. I just got kind of attached to Blackie. I get attached to animals."

"It's okay. You can visit him."

"You're right," she says with a forced smile.

"I know. It's not the same. Let me take this bag." I take the bag of food and carry it toward the door.

"Come on in," Audrey tells Claire. "Have a seat."

"I don't want to impose."

"Please. I want to talk to you anyway."

"I have his food," I say. "I'll take it out when you're ready." I put the bag of food by the door and go back to Lilah.

After Claire sits down on the sectional, Lilah sits down next to her and I sit next to Lilah.

Audrey introduces them.

Blackie leaves Claire's arms and walks over to sit in Lilah's lap.

Lilah's face lights up and she hugs him.

"Oh. He likes you," Claire says. "I'm so glad he made a friend."

"We're best of friends," Lilah says.

"So. Claire," Audrey says. "I'm hoping you're planning

to come back to work for us."

"Oh," Claire says nervously. "I don't know if Mr. Fields will allow it."

"Give me his number," Audrey says. "I'll call him and make a personal request."

"I'll do that," Claire says. "If you're sure you don't mind."

"It's settled then," Audrey says. "Be thinking about when you can come back."

"I can come back whenever you need me," Claire says. "Do you need me to do something right now?"

"No. Of course not. You've got to get home and get settled back in. Come back in a day or two."

"I'll be here tomorrow," Claire says.

"We'll be pleased to see you," Bradley says.

We all look at him.

"What? None of us have exactly taken the time to do any cleaning."

"You've got us spoiled, Claire," Audrey clarifies, elbowing Bradley. "It's a good thing."

Lilah, her eyes wide and moist, her face pressed against Blackie's fur, looks over at Claire. "Do you think maybe you could bring Blackie when you come to work?"

"Of course I can," Claire says, smiling. "I think he would like that. He hates being left alone all day."

"So would I," Lilah says, smiling over at me.

"I'll get out some of the food. Just enough so you don't have to pack it back over here."

"Wyatt's a good man," Claire says, looking at Lilah. "You're a lucky girl."

Lilah looks at Claire in confusion.

"Actually I'm the lucky one," I say, bending over to give Lilah a kiss on the cheek.

Claire clasps her hands together beneath her chin. "This is so romantic. I'm so happy for you all and I'm so lucky to work here."

I go over to take a few cans of cat food out of the tote bag and the almost empty bag of dry cat food.

I am definitely the lucky one. No doubt about that.

FORTY-EIGHT

Lilah

THE HOUSE SEEMS empty after Claire leaves, taking Blackie with her.

I sit at the table, researching roses, but my heart isn't in it.

"It'll be okay," Wyatt says. "She'll be back and she'll bring Blackie with her."

"I know. I just got used to Blackie sleeping on my bed."

He reaches over and puts a hand over mine. "Let's go into town tonight. Have pizza."

"Leave Audrey and Bradley?" I ask.

"They can come if they want to, but I don't think they'll have any complaints about being left alone."

"Okay," I say with a little smile. "You're right."

His phone rings. "It's Trent," he says.

"About the cameras."

"Yeah. He must have something. I'll put him on speaker."

"Hey Trent. You're on speaker with Lilah here."

"Hi Lilah," Trent says.

"Hi Trent."

"You must have something," Trent says.

"I do have something and it's not what I expected."

"That can't be good."

"Well. It's something I personally haven't seen before. I had to consult with my boss."

"What was it?" I scoot my chair closer to Bradley's, keeping my gaze locked on his.

"Well. Let me see if I can explain it."

"We're listening."

He takes a breath. "Take me off speaker."

"Okay." Wyatt takes him off speaks and holds the phone up between us so can both hear.

"You've got some time gaps."

Wyatt looks at me. "Gaps? When someone came in and took the dog."

"Yes. My best guess. Someone put a scrambler on your Internet."

"Wait. What?" Wyatt holds the phone out, staring at it.

"It's quite sophisticated," Trent explains. "They just flip a switch and your Internet goes off. Everything stops recording. Then it comes back on and you don't even know it happens."

I feel heat rising in my cheeks. It's the same feeling I had just before I tossed the glass of wine in Bernice's face. Only this time there's no target. No one to throw anything at.

"How?" Wyatt asks. "How would he get past the cameras to begin with?"

"I'm thinking he's doing it remotely. Probably has the scrambler installed somewhere in the house. Just flips a switch and walks in the door."

"He doesn't have the code," I murmur, knowing it's a detail that doesn't matter.

"She means the door lock code to get inside the house."

"Digitized codes are so easy to override. If you're going to get anything other than an actual key, get the fingerprint ones."

"Now he tells us," I say.

"So, Trent," Wyatt says. "Are you telling us that someone pla—"

"Wyatt," Trent says. "Assume your walls have ears."

"Okay. Just walked right in without being detected?"

"Yes. That's what it looks like."

"Wait." I press my fingers against my brow. "But we're here. It's not like we're not home when he does it. We're right here."

"Any ideas, Trent?" Wyatt asks.

"Again. This is my best guess. Not being there to see for myself. But he probably has cameras of his own."

A chill runs down my spine. "What do you mean?"

"Cameras are so small now. They used to call them nanny cams, but now they're everywhere. He could have cameras anywhere. A power outlet. A digital clock. A smoke detector. Even an air vent."

With goosebumps on my skin, I look at Wyatt. "How do we find out?"

"You need someone with the right equipment to find out."

"When can you be here?" Wyatt asks.

FORTY-NINE

Wyatt

A FEW HOURS LATER, we sit in the pizza shop.

Lilah next to me. Audrey and Bradley across from us.

Blue checkered faux leather table cloths on the tables. Worn blue leather booths. Eighties music streaming from a jukebox in the background.

It's crowded as always. Touted as the best pizza in Whiskey Springs. Probably goes along with being the only pizza in Whiskey Springs. Still. It's good. Better than anything I ever found in Boulder as a college student dedicated to finding the best pizza, even if I did commute.

Commuting didn't mean I didn't stay over at friend's houses on a frequent basis.

Biscuit, on his leash, sits beneath the booth.

We get a few looks about that, but when the owner says it's okay, it's okay.

There's no way we were going to leave the dog alone at home or even in the truck.

"So please explain," Bradley says, "why we couldn't talk at the house or in the truck."

I lean forward, my elbows on the table. A quick glance at Lilah's drawn face.

"I talked to my friend Trent in Boulder."

"Right," Bradley says. "You told me about him."

"I gave him access to our cameras." I glance at Audrey. "Apologies for not asking your permission first."

Audrey shakes her head. "No need. We're all in this together."

I take Lilah's hand and lace my fingers with hers.

"He thinks he has an explanation for what's been happening. Not all of it, but an explanation for how someone got in the house without us knowing it and walking out with Biscuit."

"How?" Bradley asks. "We were all home."

"We were. But we were upstairs."

"He probably has cameras on us," Lilah says.

Audrey looks at her sister. "Cameras in our house? Watching us?"

"Yes. Tiny spy cameras."

"That would explain a lot," Audrey says, rubbing her arms. Bradley puts an arm around her and pulls her close.

"So he's spying on us. But that doesn't explain how we couldn't see him on our cameras."

"Trent thinks he has a scrambler somewhere in the house. He can turn it on and off remotely."

"A scrambler," Bradley says. "Son of a bitch."

"What does that mean?" Audrey asks.

"It means he can turn off our Internet anytime he wants to," Lilah says with a hint of venom in her voice.

I squeeze her hand. "It leaves time gaps on our cameras. Time gaps we don't notice."

"Why?" Bradley asks. "Why go to so much trouble?"

"He wants us out," Audrey says flatly.

"I don't understand." Bradley says with heat. "Why not just offer to buy the house? Or something. Anything. Anything that's legal. Not all this stealing the dog crap and sneaking around leaving notes at the door."

Lilah and Audrey exchange a look. Lilah nods, but Audrey shakes her head.

"They need to understand," Lilah says to her.

"It won't matter," Audrey says.

"It could matter," Lilah insists. "It matters."

"What are you not telling us?" Bradley asks.

Audrey sighs. "I don't see why it matters."

"How can it not matter?" Lilah asks. "Tell them. Just tell them and you'll see."

"Audrey," Bradley says, kissing her on the top of her

head. "If you know something that could help us solve this thing, maybe you should consider telling us."

Lilah crosses her arms. "It matters."

Our conversation comes to a halt as the server comes and takes our order. Takes her time pouring water into our glasses.

"Can I get you anything else while you wait?" she asks. "Some breadsticks?"

"We're good, Maribelle. Thank you," Bradley says.

"You know her?" I ask, looking over my shoulder at the girl, not more than eighteen, walking away.

"He knows everybody," Audrey says.

"I know. It's just... You should really run for sheriff."

"Audrey gets money for living in the house," Lilah blurts.

We all look at her.

"How much money?" Bradley asks, looking at Audrey.

"A lot," Lilah answers for her.

"No," Audrey says. "I told you not to tell anyone. I need to get out. Bradley. Please let me out of the booth."

Bradley stands up while Audrey takes off toward the bathroom.

"I should go," Lilah says.

"Before you go," I say. "Tell us how much money we're talking."

"She doesn't want me to tell anyone. It's her inheritance. I overstepped."

"Wait," I say. "You're right. This could mean something. This could mean whoever is doing this wants the inheritance money for himself."

"Exactly," Lilah says.

"How much money?" Bradley asks, keeping one eye on the bathroom door, watching out for Audrey.

"It's an annual stipend for as long as she lives in the house."

Bradley nods his head. "She told me she has to live in the house. Didn't really say why."

"Her husband left everything else to a child he has with someone else," Lilah says. "She didn't know about this child until after Thomas's crash. She lost everything. Even the house they lived in. This house is the only inheritance she got."

"How much money?" Bradley asks again.

"It's not our business," I say. "What matters is someone wants her out. Someone who thinks they have a claim to the house."

"It would have to be someone related to Albright in some way," Bradley says.

"Seemingly." I agree. "Why else would they think they have a claim?"

"Could be related to Thomas. Could be the child."

"Can't be," Lilah says. "The child is maybe three-years-old. At most. There's no way the mother could get up here to do this."

"Someone related somehow," I say.

"I need to go check on Audrey," Lilah says.

I stand up to let her out of the booth.

"She's coming back," Bradley says with obvious relief.

I figure there's going to be hell to pay, but Audrey climbs back in the booth, her expression blank. Her eyes are a little red, but that's it.

She looks from Lilah to me to Bradley.

"A million dollars," she says, keeping her gaze on Bradley's. "A million dollars goes into my account every year."

No one says anything.

Lilah was right. Lilah was so right. This changes everything.

A whole lot of people would go to a whole lot of trouble to get their hands on a million dollars every year. It would have nothing to do with living in the house. Nothing at all. Most people would live in a hovel for a million dollars a year.

The stakes just got a whole lot higher.

Along with the stakes getting higher, so does my resolve to keep Lilah safe.

No matter what it takes.

FIFTY

Lilah

"Thank you," I mouth to my sister.

"So now you know," Audrey says, keeping her gaze down.

"Thank you for telling us," Bradley says.

"It doesn't change how I feel about the house." Audrey looks back up at Bradley, searching his eyes. "Or you."

"I know," he says. "Why would you even think that?"

"Because…" Audrey says. "I just don't want you to think the worst of me.

Hearing Audrey say that out loud, I realize that particular fear must be something that runs in my family. It's how I feel about telling Wyatt that I could be arrested for throwing wine in Bernice's face.

I feel ill just thinking about it.

Maybe it's not that big a deal. The guys are looking at Audrey like they don't understand how she could be worried about them thinking badly about her for this.

But it's nothing she did.

She inherited the money.

I *did* what I did.

It's all on me.

"Lilah," Wyatt asks. "Are you okay?"

"Yes." I force a smile and hope it comes out less wobbly than it feels.

"The pizza's here," he says.

"Okay. I was just lost in thought."

He puts an arm around me. "It's going to be okay. "Whatever it is. We can handle it."

"I know." I catch Audrey looking at me questioningly. I haven't even told her, but she knows something's up. She knows there's something I haven't told her.

"Trent's coming up in the morning," Wyatt tell them as we eat our pizza.

"He's a good guy," Bradley says. "But. We still won't know who's doing it."

"We'll do the stakeout again," Wyatt says. "It didn't work last time, but I think it can."

I listen to them talk while I eat a slice of cheesy pizza.

Things were supposed to be less complicated here than in Houston.

But instead of peacefulness, I get a different kind of trouble.

As we're finishing up, Biscuit comes out from under the table.

"Come on Audrey," Bradley says. "Let's take Biscuit outside."

"I'll take care of the check, then we'll join you outside," Wyatt says. "You think Audrey's going to be okay?" he asks me after they're out of earshot.

"I think so. She'll be cross with me for a while. But I still think you needed to know just how much is at stake."

"I agree. It changes things to my way of thinking."

"Mine too. I don't think it's something we can minimize."

"I never minimized it, but this takes it to a whole other level. Kidnapping Biscuit showed me just what a dangerous game he's playing."

"You're worried that he'll escalate."

"I am," he says, looking into my eyes. "I'm not letting you out of my sight until the son-of-a-bitch is behind bars."

He makes me feel safe. No doubt about that.

But the way he says it, tells me he doesn't tolerate anyone who doesn't uphold the law.

If he knew what I'd done. If he knew that I almost got arrested, he might not look at me the same way.

I can't tell him.

I can't tell him and I can't not tell him.

CHAPTER
FIFTY-ONE

Wyatt

WHILE THE LADIES are downstairs sitting on the sectional with Biscuit, Bradley and I search the house from top to bottom.

It's creepy knowing that someone is probably watching our every move, but I'm with Audrey. We're not giving him the satisfaction of running us out of here.

Some ass hat has decided that he can run us off and claim the house and the stipend for himself.

I need to talk to Audrey. See if she can contact her attorney. Find out what the contingency plan is in the event she no longer lives here.

There has to be one. No one sets something up like that without a contingency plan. What if she hadn't come? What would happen to the house and money then? There has to be a chain for what happens next.

Finished going through the house, Bradley and I join the ladies downstairs.

I lean close to Lilah, recognizing that the walls have eyes and ears, so only she can hear me.

"He probably knew we were watching for him when we were doing our stakeout."

She nods. "That's how he knows when to show up."

"I guess we should wait until after Trent comes and finds the cameras tomorrow."

"And the scrambler."

"Is that a car?" Audrey asks as headlights shine through the window shades.

No one says anything as we listen for the car. Wait for them to realize they took a wrong turn, circle around, and head back the way they came. It happens sometimes. People out sightseeing drive up here, not realizing it's a private driveway.

But the car doesn't circle around and turn around. It stops. Whoever is driving turns off the motor.

Biscuit sits up and a low growl rumbles deep in his throat. Audrey puts a hand on his harness.

"Who would be coming here this time of night?" Lilah asks.

"Stay here," Bradley says as he and I get up to go to the door.

We wait while someone gets out of a car and walks toward front stairs.

"We should have a weapon with us," Bradley says.

"I have one," I say. "It's upstairs."

Bradley scowls at me. "Might be a good time to have it on you."

"Maybe."

We wait until the person knocks.

I hang back out of sight while Bradley opens the door to a man who at first glance is obviously from the city. He's got a slick haircut. Khaki slacks. A white button-down shirt.

I immediately don't like his looks. He looks like one of those guys who thinks he's better than everyone else because he lives in the city.

"You get turned around?" Bradley asks, looking deceptively friendly, but I see the coiled tension running through him just below the surface. He's in protective mode. We both are.

"No," the man says. "I think I'm in the right place. I'm looking for Lilah Sinclair."

I step forward. "What's your business with her?"

"I'm her boyfriend."

FIFTY-TWO

Lilah

Sitting next to Audrey while the guys answer the door, I barely breathe. I have a really bad feeling about someone driving up this time of night.

Has whoever's been leaving the notes finally just decided to drive up here and threaten us out in the open?

Whatever it is, it can't be good.

But then I hear *his* voice. The man I've tried so hard to forget. The one who caused me so much upheaval in my life.

Trey.

If it weren't for the cloud hanging over my head about

what Beatrice might or might not do, I'd be grateful to him. Grateful for shaking me out of my comfort zone and getting me here.

Hearing his voice, everything inside me just freezes.

I slowly stand up.

"Lilah," Audrey says. I ignore her and take a step forward.

Wyatt turns to face me and I see the disappointment on his face.

I shake my head, but the damage is done.

Bradley is the one who steps in.

"Lilah," he says. "Is this true?"

"No," I say.

"Just let me talk to her," Trey says. "We had a misunderstanding."

I don't move. Instead my gaze strays back to Wyatt. I try to plead with him with my eyes, but he looks away.

Audrey steps in front of me and addresses Trey. "You can talk to her in the kitchen. For ten minutes."

I look at Audrey.

"Brianna told me what he did," she says to me. "If you don't want to talk to him, we'll send him away."

I look from her to Bradley to Wyatt.

Wyatt seems to be the only one who doesn't know the whole story.

He looks confused now. But he hasn't moved. He still stands between me and Trey, even if he is off to the side a bit.

"I'll talk to him," I say.

"Come outside with me," Trey says. "So we can talk in private."

"I'm not going outside with you. I'll talk to you in the kitchen. Or you can go."

Trey hesitates. I mostly hope he just turns around and leaves. I hadn't planned on ever talking to him again.

But instead he steps inside the door.

With a sigh, I turn and go into the kitchen, not caring if he follows or not.

More than halfway hoping he doesn't.

But he does. He follows me.

I notice that he doesn't take off his coat and unlike the cocky expression he'd worn when he first came to the door, he looks a little uncertain now.

He's surrounded by people who are obviously looking out for me and from the looks of Bradley and Wyatt, they are more than ready to toss him out on his ear.

I found Wyatt handsome from the first time I saw him, but now looking at Trey, I realize that one of the things that attracted me to Wyatt is that he doesn't have that polished, metro look that Trey has.

"Why are you here?" I ask.

Trey glances over his shoulder. I just raise an eyebrow at him.

"Beatrice told me what she did."

"Why would you say those things to her?" I ask, my voice low and measured.

I feel calm, not heated like I'd felt when Beatrice had baited me.

It comes as a surprise to me that I'm calm because I don't care what Trey has to say.

"I never said anything but good things about you."

I cross my arms. "Why should I believe you, Trey?"

"Because Beatrice has been chasing me for years. She wants me for herself."

"Then. Go." I wave a hand. "Be with her. There's nothing stopping you or her."

"She's with someone now. But she can't stand the thought of me being with anyone else."

"Why are you here?" I ask again, hearing the weariness in my voice. "How did you even find me?"

"It wasn't easy to find you. I'm here to bring you home."

A movement behind him catches my attention. Bradley is sitting next to Audrey, their heads bent together in a private conversation.

Wyatt is leaning against the back of the sectional, his arms crossed, watching us.

"No." I shake my head. "This is my home now."

"You can't live here," he scoffs. "Why would you even want to?"

"You can go now." I raise my chin.

"Seriously? This is how you're going to play it?" He takes a step toward me. I don't move.

But Wyatt does. He steps forward. "The lady asked you to leave."

"Lady," Trey scoffs again.

"Don't make me ask you twice."

"Fine. Stay here." Trey turns around, but before he does, he has one more comment for me. "You'll be hearing from Beatrice's attorney."

"You don't scare me Trey," I say.

But after Wyatt follows Trey to the door and locks it behind him, I collapse on the nearest chair, my knees feeling too weak to hold me up any longer.

Audrey is there. Handing me a glass of water.

"I'm so proud of you," she says.

I take the glass, my hands trembling.

I glance around, but I don't see Wyatt. Or Bradley.

"Brianna told you what happened."

"She did."

"You didn't tell me."

"She made me promise."

"Yeah. And I made her promise not to tell you." I put the glass to my lips.

"It's one of those things I needed to know about."

I put a hand over my face and close my eyes.

I hear Trey's car motor turn over. Hear his wheels on the gravel driveway. Listen as he drives off.

He's gone. Trey was here, but he's gone now.

"How did find me?" I ask.

"I don't know. But it's going to be okay."

"It's not. Beatrice is going to have me..." I lower my voice. "arrested."

"We won't let that happen."

"You can't stop it." I set the glass on the table. "I'm going to be sick."

"No. You're not. Take a deep breath."

I shake my head. Then I'm up, rushing to the powder room. I make it just in time.

As I kneel in front of the toilet, throwing my guts up, I vaguely realize that someone is holding my hair back.

Someone hands me a wash cloth for my face.

I sit back on my heels and let hot tears run down my cheeks.

"Lilah." It's Wyatt. Wyatt was here. Wyatt is the one holding my hair back. Wyatt is the one holding me close while I cry.

It's Wyatt. Wyatt is the one.

FIFTY-THREE

Wyatt

"I'VE GOT YOU," I say, holding Lilah close, rubbing little circles on her back, soothing her.

"I'm sorry. I'm so sorry he came here."

"You didn't know," I say. "You didn't have anything to do with him coming here."

She lifts her head and I look into her beautiful green eyes, so full of sadness.

"Don't be sad, Sweetness."

"I—"

Audrey and Bradley walk by, interrupting.

"We're going to take Biscuit out for his walk," Bradley says. "Then go upstairs."

"Watch your back," I say.

"We'll be okay. Take care of Lilah."

After the door closes behind them, Lilah searches my eyes.

"I need to tell you something."

"You can tell me anything."

"I need to, but I don't think I can."

"Oh Sweetie." I kiss the top of her head. "There's nothing you can tell me that would change my mind about you."

She takes a deep breath. Lets it out slowly.

"You deserve better," she murmurs.

"Whatever it is, you can tell me when you're ready."

"What if I did something very bad? Something I'm ashamed of?"

"We all do those things."

She shakes her head. "I got fired."

"Okay."

"There was a guest where I worked. It was at a theatre in Houston. A black tie event. I was serving champagne. This woman. Her name is Bernice." She stops. Takes a deep breath.

"The one Trey was talking about?"

"Yes. She... taunted me. Called me names. Told me that Trey said bad things about me."

"What Trey said doesn't mean anything."

"Well. I sort of lost it."

"What did you do?" I ask, curious about why she could possibly have done that she believes is so bad.

"I tossed a glass of wine in her face."

I look at her a moment, trying to picture that scene. Then I laugh.

"It's not funny." But a smile tugs at the corners of her lips.

I run a hand over my mouth. "It sounds like she got what she deserved."

"I'm not denying that, but I got fired over it."

"I'm actually rather thankful that you did. It got you here."

She looks away. "Did you know that in Texas, tossing wine at someone is considered assault?"

"I can't say I did."

"It's an offense with a two-year statute of limitations."

"I see."

"So. You see my problem."

"Yes. She's going to hold this over your head."

"And Trey can get her to move on it."

"I guess he can try."

Right about now, I'm wondering if I'm too late to catch that son-of-a-bitch and give him a bloody nose. Among other things. Give him a reason to think twice about threatening my girl.

It won't happen again. I can guarantee that much.

FIFTY-FOUR

Lilah

I'M FEELING SICK AGAIN.

I told Wyatt the truth. I told him the worst thing I've ever done and just how much trouble I've gotten myself into.

And right now he won't even look at me.

Audrey and Bradley come back inside and head upstairs. Laughing about something Biscuit did.

If only life were that simple again.

Someone told me once. *Wherever you go, you take yourself with you.*

It couldn't be more true.

I've come up here to a brand new place, a beautiful place, and I brought my old self with me. The old self that did something so embarrassing.

"I understand if you don't want to talk to me anymore," I whisper past the lump in my throat.

He puts a finger gently beneath my chin.

"Bernice or whatever her name was got what she deserved. Don't worry. If anyone tries to take you away from me. For whatever reason. I'll fight them tooth and nail. You don't ever have to worry about that."

"But... Two years. For two years I have to worry about them taking me back to Houston."

"They won't try it but one time."

I look at him. At the fierceness in his expression.

"But Wyatt. You're so law abiding. I don't want to be an embarrassment to you."

"Did I tell you about the time Caleb and I got arrested for climbing the water tower?"

I look at him with disbelief. "You? You got arrested?"

"And then there was the time Bradley and I got in a bar fight. Like I said. We all do things in the heat of the moment. It doesn't define who we are now."

"It really doesn't bother you? What I did?"

"It bothers me that the ass hat would threaten you. Do you love him?"

"No. I don't love him." I shake my head.

"Then the next time he comes around here, he'll leave with a broken nose. He won't try it more than once."

A warmth spreads through me.

I'd feared the worst about telling him. I'd feared that he wouldn't want to talk to me again. But now he's threatening to do bodily harm to Trey if Trey comes back around here.

"Thank you," I say.

He pulls me close against him. "For what?"

"For not judging."

"I'm proud of you, love."

A tear slides down my cheek. I think I've found the person I'm supposed to be with. A person who understands me.

Someone who stands behind me no matter what I might do.

"Now I have something to talk to you about," he says.

"What's that?"

"How would you feel if I moved in with you and Audrey and Bradley?"

"Move in? Like live here?"

"I'm already living here. I'd just bring the rest of my clothes. Make it official. We got an offer on the cabin I'm living in. They want to buy it and fix it up themselves. That leaves me free."

"I think I would like that very much. But. It's Audrey's house. We'd have to ask her."

"I know. But I wanted to ask you first."

"Yes," I say, biting my lip to keep from grinning. "Let's ask her."

The thought of Wyatt not being here is not something I want to think about.

He kisses the tears away from my eyelids. Then presses his lips against mine.

This is where I belong and this is who I belong with.

I feel like a huge weight has been lifted off of me.

Then there's a sound at the front door.

We both freeze.

"Something is out there," I say, my heart pounding dangerously.

"Stay here. I'll go see what it is."

"We should get Bradley."

"I'll be right back."

I pick up my phone and send Audrey a quick text.

Me: Someone is outside.

FIFTY-FIVE

Wyatt

I REACH the front of the house and look out the window, moving the window shade just an inch. There's no time to check the cameras and even if there was, they probably aren't recording at the moment.

I don't see anything. Just the wind tree limbs rustling in the wind.

Nothing unusual.

Then Bradley is behind me.

"Where did you come from?" I whisper.

"We have a network," he says.

"I guess we do," I say, glancing back at where Lilah

and Audrey stand together. They'd left Biscuit upstairs, but I guess no one can get to him up there. Surely not.

"What did you hear?" Bradley asks.

"Not sure."

"There's something out there," he says, looking out the other window.

"Where?"

"On the ground."

"I don't see it."

Bradley unlocks the door and opens it. I follow him outside into the cold air.

The motion light clicks on, lighting our way.

Without hesitation, he walks down the steps to pick up an envelope camouflaged by the rocks and dirt.

So he struck again. But how? No cars. No sign of anyone walking up.

"How did he get past the motion light?" I ask, mostly to myself.

"Maybe the sensitivity is too low."

"I'll change it in the morning."

We go back inside, Bradley handing me the envelope while he locks the door behind us.

"Do the honors," he says.

"Right." I walk over to the fireplace, the others behind me and carefully open the unsealed flap, like all the other notes, and pull out a folded sheet of paper.

I read the note by firelight.

There once were four little Indians. Then there were three. Which one will be first to go?

"That's enough," I say, thrusting the paper in Bradley's hands and striding toward the front door.

I throw open the locks and step outside.

"Come out you coward," I shout toward the trees. "Come out and show yourself. Be a man."

"Wyatt," Bradley says, coming out to stand next to me. "He's long gone."

"How?" I ask. "How is he long gone?"

"I don't know. Let's go check the recordings. Maybe there's something there."

"Right." I follow him back inside, but I already know there won't be anything on the recordings.

The coward has it figured out. He's figured out a way to leave us notes without showing himself. And now he's threatening us.

It has to stop.

Tomorrow Trent will be here and we'll have another piece of the puzzle.

We'll get this figured out and whatever son-of-a-bitch is doing this is going to find himself in jail.

Or the infirmary. Infirmary first, I vow to myself. Then jail.

CHAPTER

FIFTY-SIX

Lilah

I WAKE in the middle of the night to find Wyatt sleeping in the chair.

He'd promised me he would stay a little while, then he'd go to his own room.

He can't possibly be comfortable sleeping in that chair like that.

I contemplate waking him up. But if I do, he'll go across the hall to his own room.

I selfishly don't want him to go. Even if he is uncomfortable.

Lying very still and quiet, I listen to the river rushing in the distance. To the sound of a wolf howling in the distance.

No cars. No trains. No distant roar of civilization.

We're isolated out here. I know civilization isn't too far away, but it's too far away for us to hear any signs of it out here.

I haven't even heard a siren since I got here. Not even one.

So now, after tonight, Wyatt knows everything.

He knows that Audrey is getting a million dollars a year to live here in this cabin.

He knows that I could go to jail anytime in the next two years for assaulting someone with a glass of wine. Just the liquid. Not the glass. Unfortunately it doesn't seem to matter that it was just liquid. It still counts as assault.

And yet none of that seems to matter to him. He's still here.

In fact, he wants to move in.

I don't think Audrey will mind. As long as I'm happy, she'll be okay with it.

Wyatt and Bradley are close so there won't be any animosity between the two of them.

Wyatt didn't say how long he'd live here. Just that he needs a place to live at the moment.

It's good enough for now.

I wouldn't blame him for doing the opposite. For

getting out of here. There's so much going on. With the threatening notes at the door. With my ex-boyfriend, using that word loosely, showing up unannounced at the door. With me living under the threat of being arrested.

Why would anyone subject themselves to this on purpose?

Me? Sure. Audrey is my sister. It's what family does for each other.

But Bradley and Wyatt aren't family.

I don't really see why either one of them would put themselves through this willingly.

I'm falling hard for Wyatt.

One glance at him and my heart skitters.

His nonjudgmental attitude toward me makes me feel even more for him.

Maybe it's time I stop trying to hold him at bay and start letting him know how I feel about him.

If my past doesn't bother him, maybe it's nothing I should worry about either.

"How long have you been awake?" he asks, startling me.

"Not long," I say. "How did you know?"

"You're being too quiet."

"Are you saying I'm a noisy sleeper?"

"Not at all." He shifts, sitting up in the chair.

"I know I don't snore," I say. "My sisters would have delighted in telling me."

"You don't snore," he says. "But when you're awake, I can't even hear you breathing."

"Well," I say. "You don't snore either."

"That's good to know."

"I'm sure someone would have told you," I say.

"Don't know who it would be. It's been a long time since I slept in the same room with anyone."

I can't help but wonder if I should believe him or if he's just saving my feelings.

"You can't possibly be comfortable in that chair," I say.

"Can't say it's much of a bed. Why aren't you sleeping?"

"I don't know. Edgy, I guess."

"There's a lot going on." He sits up. "Want me to come over there? Keep you company?"

"Why would you do that when you have a comfortable bed?"

"Solidarity?"

"You have a kind heart, Lilah Sinclair. Why don't I come over there and keep you company?"

I pat the bed. "I would have asked, but I didn't want to be too forward."

He laughs and gets into the bed on the other side.

"Come here," he says, pulling me into his arms. "You're safe."

I snuggle into his arms, pressing my cheek against his chest.

"I know."

If I don't know anything else, I know I'm safe with Wyatt.

FIFTY-SEVEN

Wyatt

IT'S MID-MORNING. A bright sunshiny summer day in the mountains.

Trent started in the kitchen. By the time he finishes scanning the downstairs area, he's found four tiny spy cameras. All hidden away in places we would never look. He leaves them in place on the outside chance that we're being watched at the moment.

As far as anyone can tell at an easy glance, everything is normal. He's wearing what looks like an exterminator uniform. Carrying an exterminator canister on his back. But his wand is actually a bug and spy camera detector.

Lilah sits at the kitchen table working on her flash cards. Audrey is sitting on the sectional in front of the fireplace drawing lines on a pad of graph paper. Closet designs.

Bradley is out back chopping some kindling.

"He had this place well covered," Trent says, keeping his voice low. "We'll check upstairs, then we'll check outside and your cars."

"Headed upstairs," I say so the girls can hear.

"Okay," Audrey says easily. "Do what you need to do."

"Yes ma'am," Trent says. "We'll have these pests out of here in no time."

I smile over at Lilah as we start upstairs.

Trent's wand lights up in every bedroom and he takes a photograph of each camera.

The hallway, though, is clear.

"Where do we look for the scrambler?" I ask him.

"Is there an attic?"

"Has to be," I say, looking behind us down the hallway. "Looks like access might be there." I point to a square in the ceiling.

Standing beneath it, Trent points his wand at it. The light goes off. "Found it," he says. "Got a ladder? We can disable it."

"I'll be right back."

Three minutes later I'm back with a ladder.

Trent scurries up like he's done this a thousand times.

"Pretty sophisticated equipment," he says.

"Can you disable it?"

"Yep. He won't even know it."

"Now that's the way to do it."

"You betcha."

Two seconds later, he's coming down the ladder. "You need something else?" I ask.

"No man. It's done. The scrambler is scrambled."

"Impressive."

"Ready to head outside? Check around. See what's he's got in your vehicles."

"Sure."

"I'm going to send you a file with the location and images of all the cams."

"What about our cameras? You think he's watching them?"

"I doubt it. He's got his own system. Doesn't need yours."

"What do you recommend we do now? With this information?"

"I think you'll figure it out."

"What would you do?"

"Business as usual. Watch your own cameras. With his scrambler off, he's going to slip up. Won't be long."

He finds bugs and trackers in our trucks and the girls' cars. A couple of outside cameras.

We walk down to the river and look back up at the house.

"Whatever this guy is up to, he's serious about it." Trent shifts his canister.

"He had the cameras in place before Audrey moved in?"

"I'd say yes. But they're definitely the latest technology."

"I don't know how to thank you."

"As you can see by the disguise, I've done this before. It's not unusual."

"How much do I owe you?"

"You don't owe me anything. Buy me lunch next time you're in Boulder."

"I'll buy you lunch right now."

"And I'd take you up on it, but I've got to get back. Raincheck."

We walk around the house to his truck where he loads up his equipment. He really does legitimately look like an exterminator.

We clasp each other on the shoulder. "Thanks, Man."

"You betcha. Don't forget to let me know when you're in town."

I watch him drive away.

Now. Now we're going to find out who the son-of-a-bitch is that's been leaving these notes and kidnapping our dog.

FIFTY-EIGHT

Lilah

TAKING BISCUIT WITH US, the four of us walk down to the rushing river where Wyatt explains what Trent found.

"He really did have a scrambler in the house," Bradley says, running hand through his hair.

"He really did. And he's watching everything we do. Listening to everything we say."

"What do we do now?" I ask, feeling the need to do something, anything, running through my veins.

"We wait. The next time he comes to the door to leave something, we'll know it. Our cameras will be working."

"It's hard to be patient," I say watching Biscuit sniffing along the edge of the riverbank.

"Lilah has very little patience," Audrey says.

"They're a good match," Bradley says and we all look at him. "What? Wyatt doesn't have a lot of patience either."

I look at Wyatt. "I haven't noticed."

"You will," Bradley says, earning a jab from Audrey's elbow.

"They're like an old married couple," Wyatt says, looking pointedly at his brother. "Thinking they have everything all figured out."

Bradley crosses his arms with a smug expression.

"Wyatt's moving in," I say, deciding this is as good a time as any to let them know.

"I thought he already had," Audrey says.

Wyatt and I exchange a look. "I guess that means she's okay with it," I say.

"I guess so."

"While we're exchanging news," Audrey says, looking up at Bradley.

"I thought we were going to wait," Bradley says.

"You just want to torture your brother," Audrey says.

Bradley winces. "Audrey and I are getting married."

"What?" I look at my sister for confirmation.

"Not yet. We have to go get a ring and we're going to wait. Maybe until... I don't know."

"Maybe the holidays," Bradley says. "When your family can be here."

"Our family can come anytime," I say.

"We want this... mess to be behind us before we start planning," Audrey says.

"I'm so happy for you." I give my sister a hug. "Congratulations to both of you."

Biscuit runs to us from the riverbank, wrapping us all together in a circle with his leash.

Wyatt takes my hand. "I think Biscuit just gave his approval."

"We're all one family now."

Bradley goes about unwrapping us and Biscuit charges back toward the house, tugging him along with him.

"I guess we're going back inside now," Audrey says.

"I guess so," I say, walking along behind them, holding Wyatt's hand. "It's such a beautiful day."

"Do you feel like painting?" he asks.

"I should.... But not really. I don't want to be away from the house right now."

"I'll come out with you."

"I'm kind of on a roll with my flower project right now."

"Did you talk to Audrey about it yet?" Wyatt asks.

Audrey looks back at us over her shoulder. "Audrey says you can put it wherever you want to. It's your house, too."

"Did she just refer to herself in the third person?" Wyatt asks me.

"She means well," I say. "You'll see. She's going to be your sister."

Does that mean Wyatt is going to be my brother?

No. Absolutely not.

I look at him sideways. Not Wyatt. Bradley. Bradley will be my brother.

"You're thinking too much," he says.

I don't even question how he knows that.

It doesn't matter. He's right.

CHAPTER
FIFTY-NINE

Wyatt

THE FOUR OF us stay close together the rest of the day.

We work on our own projects. Make homemade pizza. Then settle down on the sectional to watch a movie.

I have the iPad open, watching the cameras. Knowing someone has been randomly turning our cameras off is unsettling. But knowing that won't be happening again is empowering.

Now if someone comes up to the door, we'll know it. We'll see it on the cameras.

Lilah sits snuggled up beside me while the movie plays. It's a comedy, something we all need.

Something on the cameras catches my attention.

Just a bird. Flying the length of the front porch before heading back to the trees.

"See something?" Lilah asks.

"Just a bird," I say. I'd turned the sensors up all the way, but it still wasn't enough for the bird to kick on the exterior motion lights. It's almost like it flies just under the detection range.

A few minutes later, a bird flies around by the back door. Same bird? Surely not. Again. The light doesn't click on.

I decide it's the angle. Maybe I'll add another light to cover any direction someone could use, including coming up from the side of the house.

When the movie's over, Biscuit stands up and barks once.

"I know. I know. You want to go outside," Bradley says, disentangling himself from where he'd been curled up with Audrey. He tells Biscuit. "Go put your leash on. Uncle Wyatt did a good thing getting that leash."

"I have uncanny timing," I say.

Lilah looks at me sideways. "Is that so?"

"Sometimes. Sometimes I do." I kiss her on the cheek.

Audrey goes to the door to keep an eye on her fiancé while he secures the leash on the dog and takes him outside.

"We need to order new door locks," I whisper to Lilah.

"I think Audrey and Bradley are working on that."

"Good."

Bradley comes back inside a few minutes later with dog in tow.

"Anybody recognize this?" he asks.

"What now?" Lilah asks with a groan.

"What is it?" Audrey asks, looking at what is in Bradley's hand, but not touching.

"It's a flower. A daisy. Like the one on the dining room table."

"The one I gave Lilah. Which is still there." I glance in that direction to be sure.

"But this one has a ribbon around it," Audrey says, looking at us.

"I didn't do it," I say, standing up and walking over to get a better look. "Where was it?"

"On the back porch. Just to the left of the door."

"Son-of-a-bitch," I say. "How? How did he—?" I stop myself. I know how. "There's a blind spot someone can use if they come up along the side of the house."

"How did you figure that out?" Bradley asks.

"By accident. Watching a bird's flight path."

"He must have walked up through the woods," Audrey says.

"Is there a note?" Lilah asks.

"No note this time," Bradley says.

"He didn't need one," Lilah says. "His meaning is pretty clear." She looks at me.

"You're right." I know she's right even though I don't

know what that meaning is. Whatever it is, it has something to do with me and her.

Maybe he knows I'm moving in. Maybe he knows I gave her a flower like this. A whole lot of maybes.

Whatever it is, it needs to stop.

"I'm going into town tomorrow," I say. "Get some more motion lights."

"I can order them," Lilah says. "Have them here in a day or two."

"Let's look," I say. Now that I think about it, I don't think anyone needs to be left alone here right now. And I don't think we need to all leave the house either. Not when someone obviously has access.

No one and nothing is safe right now.

Like Lilah, I'm feeling edgy. I'm worried that the son-of-a-bitch is going to do something stupid. Something to try to hurt Lilah.

I think that's what the flower means. I think it, but I don't say anything. Not yet. I'm not an alarmist. But I'm a cautious man and I'm not leaving Lilah alone tonight.

If I'm lucky she won't let me sleep in the chair.

Lilah

"You can sleep in my room, but you can't sleep in the chair."

"Where would you have me sleep?" Wyatt asks.

We're alone in my bedroom with the door locked.

Audrey and Bradley are in Audrey's bedroom with Biscuit, their door locked, too. This is no way to live.

It's a little hard to complain though. Being locked in my bedroom with a handsome man.

Definitely hard to complain and no one will hear me doing it. Not with any seriousness anyway.

"You can sleep in the bed," I say, deciding which pajamas to pull out of my dresser.

"Milady is very kind."

I smile, biting my lip. "As long as your intentions are honorable."

"Nothing else." He sits down to take off his boots. "Do you think we should let our siblings have their wedding first or would you like to have a double wedding?"

I freeze. Slowly closing the drawer, my favorite pajamas in my right hand.

"I think maybe I heard you wrong." Turning around, I lean back against the dresser, my heart pounding frantically in my chest.

He walks toward me, slowly, his gaze intently locked onto mine.

He stops inches in front of me. His expression unreadable. Intense.

"Lilah," he says. "I've known I wanted to marry you since the moment I first saw you across the meadow."

I swallow. My breath coming in little gasps.

I keep one hand on the dresser behind me to keep myself steady.

"What took you so long to tell me?" I ask, my voice barely more than a whisper.

He wraps his arms around me and kisses me until I'm weak in the knees.

Then, as though he can sense how weak he makes me, he picks me up bridal style and carries me to the chair.

"Lilah," he says, kneeling in front of me. "Will you marry me?"

"Are you sure you want to marry me? I could be arrested at any time."

"If you are, I'll be right there with you, every step of the way."

"You deserve better," I say, my gaze searching his.

"There is no one better," he says. "There's no one better for me. You're it."

"I feel the same way."

He grins. "Then... Yes? You'll marry me?"

"Yes," I say, biting my lip. "I'll marry you."

He kisses me again, pulling me into his lap, making me breathless.

A limb bumps against the window, making me jump.

"What about the stalker?" I ask.

"We'll figure out who's doing it. I know where the blind spots are now." He kisses my forehead. "Whatever happens, we're in this together."

I nod. "You don't think it's weird? Your brother and my sister?"

"I think it's efficient."

"Efficient. That's a good way of looking at it."

He kisses me again.

"Wait?" I put a hand on his chest. "Am I just a convenience for you?"

"Lilah Sinclair. You're everything to me."

"And you're everything to me. Should we keep it a secret? Let Bradley and Audrey have their moment?"

"We can if you want to, but Bradley always knows."

"How does Bradley know?"

"I told him that day I met you. I told him you're the girl I'm going to marry."

"You did not."

"Scout's honor. You can ask him."

"I'll take your word for it." I'd much prefer to take his word for it than to get anyone else involved, even Bradley or Audrey. This is between me and him.

Just us.

There are so many things we don't have figured out. So many things still unresolved.

But together he and I can get past all those things.

We can get past those things and we'll have our own happily-ever-after.

EPILOGUE

Lilah
Two Weeks Later

I'M STANDING in the middle of an area measured off with little stakes of wood stuck in the ground adorned with orange plastic streamers.

"The concrete truck is on the way," Wyatt says walking toward me.

"We're really doing this." I look toward the house, several yards away. Our flower shop, as yet unnamed, is within walking distance just as we'd planned, but it's hidden from the house by a grove of trees.

"That's right." He wraps me in his arms. "We're doing it. You and me."

"Aren't you a little bit afraid?" I ask.

"I'm not afraid. You and me. We can do anything."

Once things started moving, they started moving quickly. Wyatt, I'm learning does not waste time when he decides to do something.

"Winter's coming," I say, looking toward the mountains where clouds hover over the peaks. It's so strange that it's still summer in most of the country, but not here. Here it's about to be winter.

"You just skipping right over fall?" he asks.

"Right. You said fall is the prettiest season."

"It is. When the leaves turn colors. You're going to love it."

"I guess I'm just wondering how we're going to get flowers down the mountainside in the bad weather. Once the roads are closed."

"Drones. Bradley's idea about the drones is the best one I've heard."

"You really think drones can carry bouquets of live flowers?"

"I do. I don't think you understand how far drones have come. Other companies are doing it. We can do it, too."

"Show me," I say, pulling my jacket closer. It might still be summer, but the wind up here is perpetually cold.

"Okay." Wyatt unlocks his phone and begins typing. "Here."

He holds up his phone, showing me photos of drones.

I expected to see ugly metal drones, but instead the page he's holding up has drones that look like birds.

"Wyatt," I say quietly. "These drones look like birds."

"Birds?" He shifts so he can see the photos with me. "Birds."

Neither one of us says anything. We just stand there looking at the page of bird drones on his phone.

"Oh. My. God." I put a hand over my mouth.

"Birds," Wyatt says. "That's how he did it. He delivered the notes with a drone. A bird drone."

We just look at each other while he slowly lowers his phone.

"Let me see," I take his phone and scroll down the page. "There. This one. This is the bird we kept seeing. But it wasn't a bird."

The concrete truck rumbles up the road, coming up the curving mountainside road toward us.

"Now we know *how* he did it," Wyatt says. "All we have to do now is figure out *who.*"

For the first time, I feel confident that we're going to figure out who's been leaving notes at our door.

We know he was turning off our WI-FI when he kidnapped Biscuit. That's why the cameras didn't record.

But we haven't been able to figure out how he was leaving the notes.

We've been seeing a whole lot of birds flying around though.

"So smart," Wyatt says. "So smart we couldn't figure it out."

"But we did," I say. "We did figure it out."

He takes my hand and kisses me.

"You and me," he says. "We can do anything."

I'm starting to believe him.

"Right now we're about to lay the concrete foundation for our flower shop," I say.

"I can't wait to tell Bradley and Audrey what we figured out."

"What are we going to do about it?"

Wyatt grins. "Bradley and I are going hunting. Starting tonight. We're going to shoot ourselves a bird drone."

And then we'll know. Then we'll know who's been threatening us.

And we can get on with the business of living our lives.

Together.

"I love you," he says, giving me a kiss on the lips. "Everything about you. I always have and I always will."

And that's all I need to know.

The End.

Keep Reading for a preview of Just Melt...

AUTHOR OF JUST SURFACE
KATHRYN KALEIGH
Just
MELT
THE GRAVITY OF US SERIES

JUST MELT
PREVIEW

Chapter 1
Brianna Sinclair
Houston, Texas

I DECLARE A DATING moratorium on the Friday evening after Thanksgiving.

The weather is unseasonably cold for November in Houston.

So cold, in fact, that I'm wearing black tights beneath my beaded little black dress.

Never mix work with pleasure.

Even knowing that, I fell prey to the allure of an older

man, an attorney I've been working for for all of a week when he asks me to meet him for drinks after work.

He had such a nice smile. In his thirties, at least ten years older than me, I decide it can't hurt anything.

After all, I spent Thanksgiving alone. By myself. I've never spent Thanksgiving alone.

But my parents are in Atlanta and both my sisters are living in Colorado.

I was invited, of course. Invited to Atlanta and invited to Colorado.

But... work.

I'm sitting in a restaurant I can't afford on my salary as a temp worker, wearing a dress I never should have cut the tags off of. Never cut the tags off a dress that comes with a warning. *No returns once tags are removed.*

There are no qualifications on the tags. No exceptions. Nothing that says you can return the dress if your date doesn't show up. Even if your date asked you to a really expensive restaurant and you went out and bought this really expensive dress to wear to the really expensive restaurant with the handsome, charming boss man who didn't show up.

And there was once an old lady who lived in a shoe.

I glance at the time on my phone. I've been waiting for forty-five minutes.

Forty-five minutes.

Now I have to go. Even if he showed up now, I would look desperate for waiting this long.

The restaurant is crowded with couples and a groups of people coming out for dinner after a day with family.

The tables are covered with crisp white table clothes. Real candles. Live flowers in vases on each table.

Waiters in formal black tuxedos dart silently and efficiently between the tables, seeing to their customers' needs, often before the customers even realize they need anything. Refilling drinks. Sweeping away empty plates. No one notices them. They're simply moving furniture.

Conversations are hushed. No one speaks too loudly or laughs too loud. Not here. Not in this too expensive for working people like me restaurant.

I envy them. Not the formality of it all, but the friends and families. I envy them even though I had chosen not to be with my own family this holiday.

Just like I chose not to be with my family, I'm choosing not to date again.

I've worked in the business world long enough to know that a moratorium needs to have a specified time limit.

Well. I don't have a time limit on my moratorium.

I declare my moratorium to be until further notice. It's my moratorium and if I want it to be until further notice, then it can be until further notice.

I pull a twenty out of my handbag to cover the glass of wine I barely touched and lay it on the table.

No one notices when I get up and slip out of the restaurant.

It's almost like everyone knows I don't belong here. They don't care if I leave. Why would they?

I broke my own rule. I agreed to a date with an employer.

As I wait for the valet to bring my car around. Hand him another twenty I can't afford to spend. I get an email from the temp company that employs me.

With nothing else to do while I wait for my car, I open the email.

Another mistake in a long line of mistakes that are the building blocks of this day.

Dear Ms. Sinclair,

We regret to inform you that we no longer need your services effective immediately.

As you know, we have a zero tolerance policy against employees fraternizing with employers.

My car arrives and I don't even bother to read the rest of the email.

Last time I checked, fraternizing would involve two people. If they think I'm fraternizing, they need to check their sources.

No one showed up.

The man who asked me out must have set me up.

What a champ.

I could respond to the email. Insist that he never showed up. But that is an admission of intent. I have no defense.

Not worth the fight.

Couldn't pay me to talk to him again or to set foot in his office ever again.

Something good comes out of everything.

After I'm in my car, the valet closes my door and I take off.

This is the last Thanksgiving holiday I'll ever spend alone.

In fact, as I drive along the festively decorated streets of Houston, it occurs to me that I no longer have ties to Houston.

My parents are in Atlanta. My sisters in Colorado.

Both of my sisters are engaged to local men, so they won't be moving back to Houston.

It's like adding insult to injury after a long day of disappointments to realize that I no longer belong here.

I've overstayed my welcome.

Without giving myself time to second think myself, I dial my sister Audrey's phone.

JUST MELT
PREVIEW

Chapter 2
Caleb Winslow

"I'm out," I say, folding my cards and placing them face down on the table.

We're sitting at the dining room table at the widow Audrey's house. Correction. Audrey, my brother's fiancé.

The wind is howling outside. The wind always howls at nine thousand feet in elevation in the Colorado Rockies just outside of Whiskey Springs where both my brothers now live. With the widow Audrey and her sister Lilah.

"Seriously?" Bradley says. "You're letting Wyatt win

again?" Bradley is the oldest of us three brothers and he's the one marrying the widow.

"I can't help it if I always win," Wyatt says. Wyatt is the youngest of us and he's marrying Audrey's sister, Lilah.

It's all one big sloppy mess, if you ask me. But they didn't ask me.

Two brothers engaged to two sisters.

Audrey and Lilah Sinclair. Both nice ladies. No doubt about that. And my brothers are happy. No doubt about that either.

Just not for me.

Audrey comes and sits down in Bradley lap. "Guess what?" she asks, putting her arms around him in an overt display of affection.

"Please tell me it's something good."

"It is." She grins. "Brianna is coming."

"To visit? Finally." Bradley looks at me. "Brianna is their sister."

"That's great news," I say. "I look forward to meeting the elusive third sister."

"We haven't seen her in months," Audrey says.

"What's happened?" Lilah says, pulling off her headset and looking over the back of the oversized sectional.

The first floor of what some call the Albright cabin, others call it the Albright estate due to its large two-story size. The first floor is open with the kitchen, dining room, and living room all spaciously arranged. The second floor has four bedrooms, each with ensuite bathrooms and walk-in closets. Audrey's room has its own spa-like bathroom, two walk-in closets, and a sitting room.

"Brianna is coming," Audrey says.

"Really? When?"

"She's flying up..." Audrey glances at her phone. "Monday."

"Monday," Wyatt looks at me. "Don't you have to be in Denver on Monday for a meeting?"

"I think so." I know so, but I can already sense where this is going.

"You can pick Brianna up at the airport. Save her having to drive up here."

"Yes," Audrey says. "That would be great. Brianna's not the best driver."

"And she always manages to get lost whenever she goes anywhere new," Lilah adds.

Great. Just great. I can already see I'm not getting out of this one.

"I don't know her. I don't even know what she looks like." It's a feeble attempt to get out of it and I know it.

Audrey and Lilah look at each other. "She looks like me with dark hair," Lilah says getting a nod of agreement from Audrey.

"It's time," Bradley says, glancing at the clock on the mantle.

"Yes. We better get going," Wyatt says, pushing back his chair.

"Where are we going?" I ask. Anywhere is better than here with them making plans for me.

"We're going hunting," Wyatt says.

"Oh." I hold up a hand. "I don't think so."

"Come on, Bro," Bradley says. "You don't have to shoot anything. You can do the spotting."

"Gave that up years ago," I say.

"I'll get the guns," Wyatt says, heading to the back door where we keep the guns.

He comes back with two shotguns.

"You're serious," I say. "What am I missing here?"

"It's just bird shot," Wyatt says, handing Audrey a small gun, the size of a pistol, but a type of gun I've never seen before. "But this is for the kill shot."

"You people are starting to scare me," I say.

I grew up around guns. I can shoot. I'm a good shot, actually. Really good. But as an adult, I choose not to hunt.

"This is a VSKP03. An anti-drone gun," Audrey says. "We have to use both."

"Wait a minute. You're shooting down someone's drone?"

"If we're lucky."

I glance over at Lilah, sitting with the big dog, a black lab, in front of the fireplace. She is apparently the only one of the bunch who has any sense.

All four of them look at me, then look at each other.

"Yes," Bradley says. "And you are now sworn to secrecy by default."

"Come on Lilah," Audrey says. "You and Wyatt are at the back of the house."

Lilah gets up and follows Wyatt toward the back door.

We all put our coats and scarves on before heading outside.

"Why doesn't Lilah have a gun?" I ask, going with Bradley and Audrey.

"We only have one of these," Audrey says. "And she doesn't like to shoot."

"Well, we have that much in common."

"Stay close to the wall," Bradley says as the three of us step out the front door and line up against the wall.

"I'm really hoping for an explanation."

"You'll get one," Bradley says.

"How do you know there will be a drone?" I ask, my hands in my pockets.

I know it's been awhile since I spent any quality time with my siblings, but this is ridiculous.

Maybe they're just messing with me.

I'm about to call it a night. Just get in my truck and head home.

But then I hear the distinct sound of a bird flapping its wings.

Both Bradley and Audrey lift their respective guns.

"Stay back against the wall," Bradley warns.

The sound of the bird is getting closer. It doesn't sound like any bird I've heard before. It's... louder. With a whirring sound.

Just as the bird sweeps beneath the overhang, Lilah lifts her gun and points it toward the bird. The whirring stops, but the bird keeps going.

That's when Bradley aims and shoots.

The sound of the gun echoes through the night.

I immediately hear the back door slam, then Lilah and Wyatt burst breathlessly out the front door.

The motion lights click on.

"Did you get it?" Wyatt asks.

"Of course."

The bird lies on the ground, just on the other side of the porch.

"You said drone," I say, my ears still ringing from the shotgun.

"Bird drone," Wyatt says, stepping out to pick it up.

"Why are we killing bird drones?" I ask. "Please tell me you have a good reason for this."

"Do you remember us talking about someone leaving threatening notes at the door?" Wyatt asks.

"You took care of that."

"It stopped for awhile, but then it started up again." Wyatt takes the bird drone inside and we follow him.

Bradley locks the door behind us, throwing two dead bolts.

Wyatt drops the bird drone on the floor and peels an envelope from its little talons.

"It comes bearing tidings tonight," he says, handing me the note.

"I don't want it."

"Read it."

Giving up on avoiding whatever this is, I take the envelope and pull out a sheet of paper.

"What does it say?" Lilah asks.

"It says *Enjoy your last holiday here. Your days are numbered.*"

"As are his drones," Lilah says with a little scoff.

"Wait a minute. How many of these things have you shot down?"

"This makes four."

"Four drones. Do you know how expensive these things are?"

"Do you know of anyone who would be using them to drop off notes like that?" Bradley asks.

"No. I do not. Isn't this a job for the sheriff?"

"He's an ass hat," Wyatt says.

"It's his job."

"Try telling him that."

Audrey kneels down, digging through the feathers. "Wyatt's friend is tracking down the serial numbers. He'll eventually find out who these things belong to."

"Trent," Wyatt says clarifies. "Trent is helping us."

I rub a hand over my eyes. What the hell has my brothers gotten into now?

"Does Brianna know what she's getting into?" I ask. Do they even understand how serious this could be? Someone is buying expensive drones for what looks like the sole purpose of trying to threaten Audrey and Lilah and possibly now my brothers away.

"No," Audrey says. "We don't want her to worry. We'll explain it when she gets here."

That's got to be a huge mistake. She needs to know. But it's not my decision.

"Okay," I say. "You've gotten me into this. I think you need to back up and tell me the whole story."

Whatever is going on sounds far more serious than they're letting on.

I don't want to be involved, but in a moment of weakness I came up here to spend an evening with my brothers who will no longer go anywhere without their women and their dog.

And this where it gets me.

"I need to know everything."

JUST MELT

PREVIEW

Chapter 3

Brianna

In retrospect, I've been preparing for this move for longer than I realized.

I hadn't renewed my lease. Instead, I've been paying month to month and I've been living a minimalistic lifestyle. My condo was furnished, so the furniture isn't even mine to begin with.

It's almost like I've been planning my getaway.

That what it feels like anyway as I board the commercial jet that will take me from Houston to Denver.

I spent the weekend boxing up all my belongings.

Everything that doesn't fit in my two oversized suitcases, got dropped off at the UPS store on the way to the airport.

Done and done.

God help me, I'm putting Houston in my rearview mirror. Didn't think I would ever do that. But these past few months of living here with no family have been just plain lonely.

It was bad enough when my older sister got married and moved out to Katy. It was one of those sudden marriages that made no sense to me. But the guy looked good on paper and the background check I secretly ran on him came out clean.

Turned out, though, that the background check missed some rather important details.

Like the baby he had with another woman before he married my sister.

This probably never would have even come out except that he, Thomas, crashed his private jet and died. All his insurance money went to the baby and the baby's mother. Even the house he'd been living in with my sister was sold out from under her and that money, too went to the child.

But Thomas's grandfather had left a house just outside of a small town in Colorado. Whiskey Springs. He left it specifically to Thomas's wife who just so happened to be Audrey.

The only stipulation was that Audrey live in the house. She doesn't own the house, but she'll live there free and clear, all expenses paid as long as she wants to.

With a one million dollar stipend deposited in her account every year.

I'd been skeptical about the whole thing when it went down, but Audrey had been determined that she had no choice but to go.

She really didn't have a choice. Who wouldn't go? She had to at least try.

Lilah and I tried to go with her, but Audrey wanted to do it on her own. Said she needed to do it herself as part of the process of learning to be single again. That didn't last long.

She'd no more than gotten to the house, not even settled in, when she met Bradley Winslow. They're engaged now.

And not long after that, my other sister, Lilah, got herself in some trouble and went up to live with Audrey in the big house.

Lilah is now engaged to marry Wyatt Winslow.

So my sisters are engaged to brothers.

"Excuse me," I say to a teenage boy with earphones on. "That's my seat."

He stands up and I crawl over into my window seat.

There's a reason I don't fly. It's self-imposed misery. The reason I haven't been to visit my sisters in the six months or so that they've lived in Colorado.

That and driving is out of the question. I rarely even take a day off. How could I possibly drive up there and back? Why would I drive up there and back?

I settle into my seat and watch the baggage handlers toss our luggage from the luggage cart into the cargo hold of the airplane.

It's raining now, so our luggage is getting wet in the process. The only saving grace is that my luggage is hard-sided.

I feel sorry for those people with cloth luggage.

I check my phone. No messages.

Send a quick message to Audrey letting her know I'm on the airplane.

Apparently Bradley and Wyatt have a third brother named Caleb who is supposed to pick me up from the airport and drive me up to Whiskey Springs.

I would have said absolutely no thank you, but I always get lost when I go somewhere new. And from what I'm told, the mountain roads are treacherous, especially since it'll be dark by the time I would be driving up to Audrey's house.

I suppose it's Lilah's house, too, since they're all living there. All four of them. My sisters and their fiancés.

I give myself a few days, maybe a week, and I'll be looking for a place of my own. Need to find myself a job first though. I'm thinking with my experience I can find a job easy enough. Give me a computer and I can do just about anything.

That's the beauty of doing temp work. I learned how to do everything. I can work in any kind of office.

"Fasten your seatbelts, folks, and prepare for takeoff.

We're going to be pushing away shortly and should have you in Denver earlier than expected."

I lean my head back against the seat and close my eyes.

I just want to be there already.

Maybe it's a good thing Caleb is picking me up. No telling where I would end up if left to my own devices. Probably end up in Wyoming or New Mexico.

The airplane starts backing out of its spot and we start driving. I'm beginning to wonder if we're going to drive all the way to Denver when the plane starts racing down the runway and we leave the ground.

Maybe driving, like Lilah had done, wouldn't have been such a bad idea, I decide as I grip the edge of the seat.

For the next few hours, it's just me and my teenage seat mate lost in his own world, headphones over his ears.

Maybe he has the right idea.

Me? I keep reminding myself.

Life changes come with strife.

If life changes were easy, everybody would do it.

JUST MELT

PREVIEW

Chapter 4

Caleb

As instructed, I get to the Denver airport, park, and find my way to the luggage carousels.

I'm on time. A little bit early, actually, but the plane, it seems, must have arrived earlier than scheduled.

Passengers are frantically grabbing their luggage, as they always do at airports, and heading out of the terminal, meeting me head on. I dodge them. A lot of families traveling together this time of year. A few businesspeople wearing their business suits.

I fit in with the businesspeople. I look like just another

businessman wearing a business suit, except I'm going the wrong direction and I'm not here for myself. I'm just here to pick someone up.

The things we do for family.

Speaking of family, my brothers have gotten themselves tangled up in some kind of mess revolving around the widow Audrey.

From what I was told, she inherited the house from her late husband's grandfather, the only stipulation being that she has to live in the house. She can't not live there and she can't sell it.

Oh. And every year she gets a million dollars deposited in her account.

Not a bad deal.

And apparently someone else knows about this arrangement. Someone who wants her out.

Someone wants her out so they can move in.

So far their tactics have been leaving threatening notes at the door. Messages, they learned after some time, left by bird drones.

One of their tactics, however, was not harmless. They kidnapped Bradley's dog, Biscuit.

As far as I'm concerned, that was taking it too far.

Biscuit was unharmed, returned unscathed a few hours after he was taken from their house, right while everyone was upstairs working on installing shelving in the closets.

Whoever was able to get into the house to get the dog,

without being recorded on their cameras, had installed their own scrambler *inside* the house.

Since no more incidents like kidnapping the dog have occurred, whoever did it must know that his scrambler has been disabled. Very likely since he had cameras planted inside Audrey's house.

Cameras that they pulled down and stored out in the tool shed.

Me? I would have pulled them out and put them down the garbage disposal or tossed them in the river. But they're keeping them for evidence even though they won't go to the sheriff with this thing.

Bradley went to the sheriff when it started, but the sheriff blew him off. Now they've decided to take things into their own hands by shooting down the guy's drones.

It seems like a dangerous game to me.

I'm not sure they see the danger.

If someone will mess with a pet, he'll mess with a person.

Something needs to be done. I don't know what it is, but I know there has to be something.

A young lady who absolutely does look like Lilah with long dark hair grabs at a black hard sided suitcase from the conveyor belt. She wobbles on high heels and the suitcase continues its path on the belt.

She's wearing a charcoal gray pencil skirt and matching jacket with an emerald green blouse peeking out beneath it.

I instantly know she's Brianna Sinclair. There is no mistaking her resemblance to Audrey and Lilah.

I cover the distance in three long strides and, stepping to her right, drag the suitcase off the belt.

"This one, too?" I ask, nodding toward the matching one coming along behind it.

"Yes," she says, watching with dismay as it rolls past her.

I grab it, too, dragging it off the moving conveyor belt.

"Thank you so much," she says, pushing her hair back. "I missed them the first time around."

"I can see why. They weigh a ton."

She looks at me with a little bemused smile.

She looks like her sisters, but she's so much prettier. At first I think it's her bow-shaped plush lips with the little smile. But, no, it's something in her eyes. So deep and such an unusual shade of teal green. Looking into her eyes, I see so much wisdom. This is not a shallow girl. This is a woman with depth. The kind of woman a man could hold a deep philosophical conversation with.

"I'm Caleb Winslow," I say.

"Brianna." She holds out a hand. Even with three-inch heels, the top of her head only comes to my shoulder.

My gaze never leaving hers, I put my hand in hers.

A connection shoots through me and for a moment I forget where we are. I forget why I'm here. Hell, I'm not even sure I remember my own name.

"I guess you're my ride then," she says.

"I guess I am." I reluctantly let go of her hand and take the two handles of her suitcases.

She moves to pick up the leather computer bag sitting at her feet.

"Let me get that," I say.

She smiles. "I'm so glad you're here," she says. "I don't know how I would have gotten this out to the rental car place."

"Your flight must have been early," I say, noticing that there are only a couple of other people at the luggage conveyor belt.

"It was. The pilot was no nonsense."

"Did you fly first class?" I ask as we make our way along the concourse.

"What? No. But it wasn't bad. The teenager sitting next to me just sat quietly and listened to music the whole time."

"Good. You never know what you're going to get on these commercial flights."

She looks at me with questions she doesn't ask.

"You hungry?" I ask.

"A little. Yes."

"Me too. If you're not in a hurry, we should stop for food before we head up into the mountains."

"Okay." We step outside and she pauses.

"What's wrong?"

"Nothing. It's just. Cooler than I expected."

"Your sisters didn't warn you about the weather?"

"They did. It's just. I don't even own a coat."

"How do you not own a coat?" I ask.

"Houston." She shrugs.

Houston. A quick reminder that she's only here to visit. And she's practically related to me with both my brothers engaged to her sisters.

I pull myself together.

It's not like I haven't seen pretty girls before.

Keep Reading Just Melt...

DON'T MISS ANY OF THE BOOKS IN THE GRAVITY OF US SERIES:

www.kathrynkaleigh.com

ALSO BY KATHRYN KALEIGH

The Gravity of Us Series

(Reading Order)

Just Breathe

Just Surface

Just Melt

Vows of Inheritance Series

(Reading Order)

Vow to Protect

Vow to Redeem

Standalone Mystery Suspense

Out of Ashes

CONTEMPORARY

(ALPINE FALLS)

Stranded in Alpine Falls

Belonging in Alpine Falls

The Spirit of Christmas in Alpine Falls

Christmas Wishes in Alpine Falls

Secrets and Second Chances

Honeymoon with a Stranger

Finding True North in Alpine Falls

A Ghost of Christmas Magic in Alpine Falls

(SILVER PINES)

The Way Back to You

Back to Where We Began

When We Were Us

(ONCE UPON FOREVER)

My Forever Guy

Our Forever Love

Forever Vows

Finding Forever

Accidentally Forever

(TRUE NORTH)

Borrowed Until Monday

Still Mine

The Moon and the Stars at Christmas

Perfectly Mismatched

On the Way to Forever

A Merry Little Christmas

On the Way Home to Christmas

It was Always You

(UNBREAK MY HEART)

Begin Again

Love Again

Falling Again

(FOR THE LOVE OF THE FLIGHT)

Just Stay

Just Chance

Just Believe

Just Us

Just Once

Just Happened

Just Maybe

Just Pretend

Just Because

(MAGNETIC NORTH)

Second Chance Kisses

Second Chance Secrets

First Time Charm

Three Broken Rules

Second Chance Destiny

Unexpected Vows

(FALLING FOR CHRISTMAS)

The Heart of Christmas

The Magic of Christmas

In a One Horse Open Sleigh

A Secret Royal Christmas

An Old Fashioned Christmas

(CITY SKYLINE BILLIONAIRES)

Billionaire's Unexpected Landing

Billionaire's Accidental Girlfriend

Billionaire's Fallen Angel

Billionaire's Secret Crush

Billionaire's Barefoot Bride

(TRULY, MADLY, DEEPLY)

The Lady in the Red Dress

On the Edge of Chance

Sealed with a Kiss

Kiss Me at Midnight

The Heart Knows

(STOLEN ECHOES)

When Cupid's Arrow Strikes

Chasing Fireflies

A Chance Encounter

(EDGE OF THE HORIZON)

The Forever Equation

Pretend Boyfriend

All our Tomorrows

Kissing for Keeps

Out of the Blue

The Princess and the Playboy

(RED LIPSTICK KISSES)

Red Lipstick Kisses and Small Town Wishes

Stolen Dances and Big City Chances

Chance Connections and Upside Down Plans

A Christmas Kiss on the Twenty-Fifth

Believe in the Magic of Christmas

ROMANTASY

(IN THE SPIRIT OF LOVE)

Spirits of the Heart

Out of Dreams and Ashes

Etched Upon the Heart

WESTERN ROMANCE

(LONE STAR HEARTS)

Wanted by a Texas Ranger

Saved by a Texas Ranger

(WHISKEY SPRINGS)

Finding Natalie

Promising Samantha

Falling for Allyson

Saving Savannah

Claiming Charlie

Rescuing Keira

Protecting Gabriella

Courting Isabella

TIME TRAVEL

(INTO THE MIST)

Written in the Wind

Scripted in the Stars

Destined in the Twilight

Promised in the Mist

Trapped in the Melody

(DRAGON'S BLOOD)

Dragon's Blood

Lavender Blue

Champagne Silver

Twilight Frost

Mountbatten Pink

(WHEN HEARTSTRINGS BECKON)

Rescued in Time

Meet me in 1879

(WHEN HEARTSTRINGS ECHO)

Messages Across Time

Falling Through to Forever

Once Upon a Winter's Spell

(BECKONED)

Before the Storm

Twist of Fate

When the Stars Align

Once Upon a Christmas

Once in a Blue Moon

A Wish Upon a Star

(BEGUILED)

When Lightning Strikes

Storm of Time

Midnight Storm

When the Moon Falls

Stormborn Angel

(SPELLED)

Time Tempest

The Heart Remembers

A Moment in Time

Moonlight Shadows

HISTORICAL

(TAPESTRY OF BLUE AND GRAY)

Shadows Beneath Magnolia Blooms

Secrets Among Southern Roses

(IT HAPPENED BY ACCIDENT)

Accidentally Alluring

Accidentally Married

(SOUTHERN BELLE CIVIL WAR)

Beyond Enemy Lines

Love Always

Hearts Under Siege

Hearts Under Fire

Away Down South in Dixie

The Reluctant Bride

Stay with Me

Jasmine Kisses

Magnolia Kisses

Gardenia Kisses

(THE QUINNS)

Wait for Me

Take Me Home

Keep Me Safe

FATED MATES

Riley's Mate

Aiden's Mate

Brayden's Mate

STANDALONE SUSPENSE

Lost and Found

All I Want for Christmas

Serenity

Courting Alley Cat

All of the books in each Series are standalone and can be read out of order. However, some books have characters from the previous stories in them.

Sign up for my NEWSLETTER to get all my romance releases, sales, Kickstarter announcements, and a **FREE** romance, SEALED WITH A KISS

www.ingramcontent.com/pod-product-compliance
Lightning Source LLC
Chambersburg PA
CBHW031607100726
47898CB00006B/1688